DETROIT PUBLIC LIBRARY
3 5674 00630363
W9-BWS-002

THE WING AND THE FLAME

ALSO BY
EMILY HANLON

It's Too Late for Sorry
The Swing

THE WING AND THE FLAME

A NOVEL BY EMILY HANLON

BRADBURY PRESS SCARSDALE, NEW YORK

William Stafford's poem, "Growing Up", from *Stories That Could Be True* by William Stafford (Copyright © 1973 by William Stafford) is reprinted by permission of Harper & Row, Publishers, Inc.

Manufactured in the United States of America. 5 4 3 2 1 84 83 82 81 80.
The text of this book is set in 11 pt. Caledonia.

Library of Congress Cataloging in Publication Data
Hanlon, Emily. The wing and the flame.
Summary: As a rare friendship develops between two teenage boys, one of them inspires a reclusive sculptor to work for the first time since his family was tragically killed.
1. Friendship—Fiction I. Title
PZ7.H1964Wk Fic 80-15082
ISBN 0-87888-168-9

FOR
CINDY

One of my wings beat faster,
I couldn't help it—
the one away from the light.

It hurt to be told all the time
how I loved that terrible flame.

William Stafford: Growing Up

THE WING AND THE FLAME

During his fourteenth summer, Eric, thanks to one old man who sculpts stone people, unlocks several secrets in time.

Return to Stoneface Mountain

The idea seemed even better in the morning. Eric dressed quickly and hurried downstairs to the kitchen, whistling.

"You using your bike today, Buddy?"

"Are you kidding? It's snowing out!"

"Good." Eric grinned, reaching for his brother's toast. "Then you don't mind if I use it?"

"Hey, that's my toast! And yeah, I do mind."

"Tough, kid. I'm using it anyway. It was mine first."

"Ma!" Buddy cried.

"Don't tease him, Eric. It'll only end up in a fight," Mrs. Nicholson said. "And put another piece of toast in for him."

"Sorry, Mom. No time. I'm in a rush." Eric gulped down half his mother's coffee.

Mrs. Nicholson frowned. "Honestly, you're home for two weeks and we never get to see you."

"Come on. If I stayed around here all the time, I'd drive you crazy. This way you think you really miss me."

"Oh, Eric . . ." She shook her head and poured herself some more coffee. "But I'll tell you one thing, I am concerned about you going to that party in Huntersville tonight. Driving on New Year's Eve is bad enough without the six more inches of snow they're forecasting."

"Mom, please . . ." Eric said impatiently. Then he sighed. "Besides, Chris and I are going with Arnold. He's got a four-wheel drive."

"That's hardly a comfort."

"Look, I have to go now. Thanks for the bike, Buddy."

"You're not really taking that bike?" Mrs. Nicholson asked.

"I have to."

"Why? Where are you going?"

"To Owen's," he said as he put on his jacket.

"To Owen's?"

Eric nodded.

"Oh, Eric, be serious."

"I am."

"Now, wait a minute. This is nonsense your biking all

the way out to Stoneface today. You and Chris have no more sense than you ever did."

"I'm not going with Chris."

"You're going alone?"

Eric nodded.

"You haven't been to see Owen for years. What's so important about biking out on a day when there's supposed to be six inches of snow?"

"Because I'll be in no shape after the party tonight to ride out tomorrow. And the day after, I go back to school."

"Then you can go out the next time you're home."

There was no way Eric could explain that urgency to his mother. It had to do with last night, sitting in the kitchen and talking with Chris until two in the morning. They were in tune, really in tune with each other as they used to be in high school when they were together all the time. But then had come graduation, different colleges and summer jobs in different states. Over the past year and a half they'd seen each other, Eric guessed, for a total of maybe two weeks . . . Last night he realized how much he missed being with Chris. And he wasn't surprised when the conversation turned to Owen and that summer five years before. They rarely spoke of that time anymore; but last night it seemed to be with them again. It was late, past midnight, when Chris said something about Eric's head always being a million miles away . . .

"Actually," Chris had gone on, "I think it all started with Owen. He got you hooked on stone people, quarries and places where the earth speaks."

Chris looked up from his beer, their eyes met, and Eric couldn't help smiling. "Not to mention caves and lights," Eric added.

"I didn't forget."

"It always seems so long ago, you know, not only the cave—Owen, that whole summer. But tonight . . ." He paused, bending a flip-top tab back and forth, and laughing self-consciously, he said, "Maybe it's the beer!"

Chris tipped his chair away from the table, was silent a moment, then exclaimed, "Hey, remember how you trekked out to Stoneface and back every day? Man, you really got mileage out of that old bike!"

"Did I ever!" Eric smiled, remembering, thinking, *The bike! I ought to bike out to see Owen again—maybe tomorrow . . .* But he didn't mention it to Chris. He figured the excitement of the idea would wear off with the beer by morning.

Eric looked at his mother now, and said, "I can't explain it, Mom. I just have to go today."

"At least drive. And take my car. Those snow tires of yours aren't worth anything."

Eric shook his head. "I have to take the bike."

"You're being unreasonable. Route 80 is terrible in winter."

"I always rode the bike out there," was all Eric said.

And before his mother could respond, he was gone.

A cold wind blew across the gray, snow-speckled sky. Eric pulled his hat down over his ears. It was going to be a long pedal out to Stoneface Mountain. There were few cars on Route 80, so Eric rode in the middle of the road as he used to on those early summer mornings when he was fourteen and biked so effortlessly, urged on by the call of the mountain, of Owen and the stone people. But there was no call today, only the lonesome whining of the winter wind as it swept across the endless, snow-covered hills, whipping across his face, making his eyes tear, his nose run and his ears sting. He began to shiver.

Maybe it's crazy to ride the bike. Maybe I should go home and get Mom's car . . . But he didn't. He couldn't. It was almost as if he needed the old bike to find his way. He tried to forget the cold, thinking instead of Owen. It had been so long since he'd seen him. They used to run into each other a lot in town before Eric went to college. Those meetings had always seemed like coincidences, but as Eric thought about them now, he knew they weren't.

It was the only way Owen could see me after that autumn. He'd never just ask me back to the mountain. Not Owen. I had to come of my own accord. But I never did. Somehow I just let Owen slide. I never thought I would. I remember meeting him in town—usually in some parking lot—and we'd talk and talk. He always made me feel so happy. I hated to say goodbye. "I'm coming out to see you real soon. I am. This time, I promise," I'd always say. And I meant it. I did. But I never went. Maybe Owen understood. I hope so—the way he'd look at me and smile. "Anytime, my friend. I'll always be there for you," he'd say . . .

And Eric pedaled harder, pushing against the wind blowing off the reservoir. He was so close to the mountain he could feel it.

Owen's jeep was parked at the fork, covered with snow, the front completely hidden in added mounds piled on by passing snowplows. *Stupid fools,* Eric muttered to himself. *Don't they know by now that someone lives out here? Don't they realize someone has to dig out that car? Well, I'll come back later with Owen's shovel.*

Leaving the bike leaning against the jeep, he started along Old Reservoir Road, making his way slowly, battling not only the knee-high snow but the bitter wind blowing off the water. Even at this pace, he estimated the walk to Owen's road would take no more than a half hour, but forty-five minutes later he still had not come to it. He stopped to rest, looking around for something familiar, but everything appeared the same: woods, woods and more woods, bare, dark trees jutting out of the white ground.

I must have missed the road, he thought, and began backtracking. Still he could find no sign a road up the mountain had ever existed. His legs were aching, and as he gasped for breath, the cold wind froze in his throat. Suddenly he plunged into the woods, deciding to forge his own path up the mountain. *I'll have to come out somewhere near the meadow.*

Tall, thin, ice covered trees swayed in the wind, moaning and cracking around him. Occasionally he'd grab hold of a limb to pull himself along. But as he made his way up the mountain, the cold grew steadily worse until he could think of nothing else. It stung his feet, his fingers and face. His whole body cried out for warmth, and he could feel himself panicking. *I should have reached the meadow by now. What if I'm not in the right place after all!*

"Owen! Owen!" he found himself calling. "Owen!"

Almost in answer to his cry came a tapping, so soft and far away it seemed to exist only in his memory. Tap, tap, pause . . . like crystal sleigh bells across the snow. The sound calmed him. *I'm in the right place. Of course I am . . .* He smiled, noticing for the first time the snow falling faster, only partially melting as it landed on his face, piling up on his eyelashes, blurring his vision. He didn't wipe it away. The woods seemed more as he remembered them through this fuzzy whiteness, absorbing him as they once had into their soft silence. The snow was so white, so smooth—*like the stone people . . . I bet that's why Owen never leaves in winter—What was it he always said about himself? . . . He hibernates—hibernates in this world like a great bear . . .* And he smiled again, envisioning himself bursting into Owen's cabin amidst a rush of swirling snow—bursting into Owen's life again, as Owen had burst into his . . . *Except it wasn't with snow—it was with feathers.* Eric chuckled, remembering the first time he ever saw Owen, rushing toward him as if from another time dimension, feathers twirling around his face . . . Eric was fourteen. It was his first spring in Fairmont.

Tap, tap, pause . . .

This time Eric stopped. "Owen?" he called softly.

Tap, tap, pause . . . The tapping grew steadily stronger. *This is insane. It's only the wind. Not even Owen could work in this cold . . .*

Tap, tap, pause . . . The sound was all about him now, pulsating through the woods like the heartbeat of the mountain. *It's Owen,* he thought. *I'm near the meadow. I must be!* He was running now, tripping in the snow drifts, the snow pushing up into his sleeves, soaking through his gloves and jeans. But he didn't notice the cold or the wet. The sky ahead of him was open. The meadow was only a few feet away. And the tapping was so loud. *It's not in my mind. It can't be. It's Owen, working. He's waiting for me—just like he said he would . . .*

"Owen!" he called as he broke out of the woods. "I'm here, Owen! I'm back!"

That Spring, Five Years Before

"WATCH OUT!" ERIC SCREAMED, PULLING CHRIS WITH him onto the curb.

An oncoming bike screeched to a halt only inches away. The rider leaped off, letting his bike crash to the street. As he did, feathers erupted from a tear in the shoulder of his down jacket, twirled around his face and landed briefly on his gray beard before drifting to the ground.

Eric couldn't help laughing.

Chris didn't. "Let's get out of here," he urged instead.

Before Eric could respond, the bike rider grasped him by the shoulders, asking anxiously, "Are you all right?" He was a tall, massive man and, in his concern, he forgot his own strength. Eric felt like a walnut being cracked open.

"Sure! I'm fine!" Eric gasped.

"Thank God." The man sighed. "I'm afraid I will crash into somebody someday. I think too much—that's my problem. And my thoughts are always in another world."

The man seemed otherworldly, appearing as he had, feathers flying, looking wild and unkempt in his ripped jacket and moth-eaten woolen cap. His ruddy, weathered face was framed with a long, wiry beard and frizzy, graying hair. But as he continued to gaze at Eric, his mouth relaxed into a smile of wonder and surprise, smoothing out the wrinkled skin, pulling it tautly across his high cheekbones, making him seem younger than he had at first appeared. Eric was staring at the man, but he couldn't help it. The man was staring back.

"We're going to be late for the movie," Chris whispered.

Eric turned abruptly. "We've got twenty minutes!" he was about to say, but the uneasy expression on Chris's face silenced him.

"Come on," Chris said, starting off the curb.

But Eric wasn't ready to leave, not just yet. *This is so crazy*, he thought, realizing he should feel awkward or embarrassed staring as he was. But he was completely at ease. *Maybe I know him from someplace.* He tried to think of where, and came up with nothing. *I'd remember if I'd ever met him. I'd never forget him . . .* There was something about the man, something Eric liked—or wanted to like. *Or is it all in my mind?* he wondered as he felt the stranger's dark, misty eyes watching, searching, absorbing, as though he were memorizing each detail of Eric's face. Eric didn't move—he hardly breathed, afraid the man, the moment, the feelings, would vanish before—before what? He wasn't sure . . .

"Hey, look, Eric—are we going to stand here all day?" Chris asked suddenly, nervously.

"Okay, okay, I'm coming . . ." Eric said. And he

turned to leave. Yet even as he did, he couldn't resist looking back at the stranger.

"I didn't mean to detain you, Eric. I'm sorry," the man said.

Eric was startled by the sound of his name spoken in the man's deep voice.

"My name's Owen, Owen Cassell. I'm sorry I've been staring at you. But you have such a resemblance to someone I know."

"I feel like I know you, too. Maybe we met someplace?"

"Fat chance," Chris muttered just loud enough for Eric to hear.

"What?" Eric shot back.

"Eric just moved here from New York City," Chris explained quickly, as though the explanation might get them moving faster.

"Then it's impossible for us to have met. I haven't been to New York in almost twenty-five years . . ."

"Hey, come on, Eric!"

"Yes," the man said, "Chris is right. You two had better go on. You'll miss your movie."

Pulling Eric by the arm, Chris started across the street. "I thought I'd never get you away from him," he moaned.

"I couldn't help it. The way he kept staring at me—who is he anyway?"

"Nobody you want to know. Take my word for it."

"Seriously."

"I am."

"Why? He looks a little weird, but he seems okay," Eric said. "And he knows you."

"Ha!" Chris laughed sarcastically. "You better believe he knows me. I wish he didn't!"

"How come?"

"I got in a lot of trouble because of him. And it wasn't even my fault. It was Arnold who did it. But just because crazy old Stoneface knows me—I get blamed."

"Who's Stoneface?"

"Him. Owen."

"Why do you call him Stoneface?"

"That's what everybody calls him. I guess because he lives on Stoneface Mountain. You should go out and see his place sometime—it's one of the seven wonders of Fairmont!"

"What did Arnold do?"

"He spray-painted his name on one of Stoneface's stone people last Halloween."

"Stone people?"

"They're some freaky statues he's made. Stoneface is a sculptor."

"How come Arnold did that?"

"Because it was Halloween. And because every time we go up there Arnold dreams about spray-painting his name across the statue of this naked woman. And because Arnold is Arnold."

Eric laughed at the thought.

"Yeah, but picture this: There's Arnold trying to spray his name by the light of this little flashlight Josh is holding, and then there's me trying to shut Bauer up, who's whistling and hooting like a fool, when all of a sudden Stoneface appears like some crazy man out of nowhere, screaming at us. It's so dark that wherever we run we trip into each other or one of the stone people or all this junk he has lying around. Then I feel this hand crushing my shoulder. Stoneface's got me in one hand and Josh in the other and he practically drags us to his cabin. I thought he was going to kill us. I don't think I've ever been so scared in my whole life. We tried to get away, but he had us both so tightly—God, my shoulder hurt for days. And then when he saw it was me—if looks could kill, I'd be dead."

"How come?"

"My father used to be friends with his son. They went to school together and whenever we go hiking on the mountain, we have to stop and see Owen. I guess that's why he was so surprised to see me that night. He gave me this whole lecture about how I was 'desecrating' his place. That's what he kept saying over and over. And of course, he went and told my father. You can imagine how thrilled *he* was . . ."

Eric looked back across the street. Owen was still there, following him with his eyes. But this time when Owen smiled once more, Eric turned quickly away. *What a weirdo!* He shivered, wondering how he could have ever thought otherwise. "Does he always look weird like that?" he asked Chris.

"Yeah. Weird."

"But does he always stare at people? Look and see if he's still watching us."

Chris turned around. "Nah. He's getting on his bike."

Eric stood in the market the next morning with the Sunday paper tucked firmly under his arm. He hoped if the woman at the counter realized he was buying something, she wouldn't mind his thumbing through the latest issue of *Sports Illustrated.* He couldn't make up his mind whether or not to buy it. If he waited a few weeks, his father could pick it up for him at half-price at the store near where he worked. *Still . . .* He frowned. *I'm tired of always waiting till it's outdated.* And placing the magazine on top of the newspaper, he started for the counter. Halfway there he changed his mind. *Nah. It's not worth it. I can wait . . .* Grumbling to himself, he turned to put back the magazine. As he did, he saw Owen standing near the doorway, watching him.

"Seems that you're trying to make a big decision," Owen said, smiling, gazing as intently at Eric as he had the day before.

Stop staring at me! Eric wanted to scream. He wanted to turn and run. But he found himself forcing a smile instead, and casually asking, "Ever read *Sports Illustrated?*"

"No. Can't say that I have."

"It's a good magazine. If you like sports. Which I do," Eric went on, all the while screaming to himself: *Shut up and get away from this creep!*

"So you've made up your mind to buy it?"

"Oh, yeah. Sure! I always buy it. As soon as it comes out—here I am, ready to buy it!" He laughed nervously. "Well, I've got to be going. My parents are waiting for the Sunday paper."

"Yes. Yes, of course. That's what I came for, too."

During the next weeks, he saw Owen several times, riding his bike or driving a beat-up old jeep which roared down the street like a hot rod, in desperate need of a new muffler. Whenever they passed, Eric pretended not to have seen Owen, but he knew Owen had seen him. He could feel his eyes on him, watching, always watching.

This is crazy! Eric would think. *This whole thing is crazy. It's not even happening. It's all in my head. And*

I'm just going to ignore it. I'm going to ignore Stoneface or whatever he's called and he'll disappear one day.

But he didn't.

≣

The first week in April—it was the beginning of the soccer season—Owen appeared at school. Eric was dribbling the ball quickly around the midfielders, making a beautiful fake past Howie Freeman, leaving nothing but an empty field between himself and the goalie.

"On your left, Eric!" Chris screamed suddenly. "Bauer's coming up on your left!"

Eric turned to find him, but instead of Bauer, his eyes focused on Owen, who was standing on the sidewalk, watching the game. Eric froze.

"Bauer's coming! Pass it to Arnold!" Chris yelled.

Eric didn't hear Chris. He didn't notice Bauer racing toward him until it was too late—Bauer and he collided, but Bauer kept his balance, stole the ball from Eric and sent him crashing to the ground.

Eric lay motionless for a few moments, his eyes closed, feeling comforted by the solid earth pressing against his body.

"Eric? Are you all right?" It was Mr. Jensen, the gym teacher.

I'm all right, but I can't get up. Not yet. He's there . . .

"Eric!" He could feel Chris's hand on his shoulder.

"Hey, what's the matter?" came a breathless voice. "I didn't push him or anything. We just hit head on."

I'm okay, Chris, Bauer, everyone. Really I am. It's just that Stoneface is out there. Chris, can you see him? He's there, isn't he? It isn't just my imagination? He tried to lift his head but as soon as he did, it began to pound and he felt sick to his stomach.

"Okay, guys, leave him alone. Chris, step back," Mr. Jensen ordered.

Maybe I should get up. I don't want to make a big deal over this. But my head hurts. And Stoneface might still be there, looking at me the way he does. Smiling.

"Eric? Can you hear me?" Mr. Jensen asked. His voice seemed far away.

I can hear you, but I can't get up yet. I have to lie here just a little longer. The earth feels so good. So safe . . . And he felt all the strength oozing out of him. He was tired, very tired . . . Then everything went black—

—Eric runs and runs with feet of lead. Something is after him, but he can't see what. It's too dark. Blackness is all around him, blackness so thick, so deep, so endless—a bottomless well of darkness through which he's plunging, falling faster and faster until he can hardly breathe.

"Help me! Somebody help me!" he screams until he feels his fall cushioned. He's floating through the darkness now, drifting, and white specks of something swarm from below him, brushing against him. Soft and downy like feathers, they fuse by the millions, changing the blackness into shades of gray, then yellow, the palest yellow. Eric reaches out to touch them and, as though he'd turned on a switch, brilliant bands of red, orange and yellow light erupt violently, swirling about him, enveloping him, spinning him as helplessly as he'd been plunged through the darkness.

"Help me! Help me!" he screams again. He screams until his throat hurts, but the screams are sucked back inside him, sucking him down, down, out of the swirling frenzy of the light, sending him crashing through the soft cushioning of feathers. He tries desperately to touch them. *If only I can catch some of the feathers,* he thinks frantically. *Then I'll stop falling.* But the feathers slip through his fingers, out of his grasp. And he keeps falling until he realizes nothing can hold him back—until he feels the pressure of the earth all about him, sucking him down further into the darkness where he can't breathe and he can't move. He's dying. He's certain of it. His life is being pressed from him . . .

Suddenly the pressure is gone. He's being lifted from the earth by large, powerful hands holding him securely but gently. And Eric knows he is finally safe. Stoneface is standing next to him wearing the dirty, torn jacket he always wears, his hand resting easily on Eric's shoulder. He smiles with his smile, staring at Eric as he always does; but Eric is no longer afraid.

Stoneface raises his arm to wave goodbye, and as he does, a blizzard of feathers bursts from his jacket.

Eric laughs. He can't help it.

Stoneface laughs, too. He waves again and turns to leave. More feathers shower them. Eric can't see Stoneface—Owen—anymore, but he can hear him laughing.

Eric is laughing, too, as he reaches out to grab a handful of feathers . . .

"Hey, look, Mr. Jensen! He's got to be okay. He's smiling." It was Bauer.

Eric opened his eyes. He was still lying on the ground where he'd fallen. He tried to push himself up, but his head hurt and he began to feel queasy again. "What happened?" he moaned.

"I think you blacked out, Eric," Mr. Jensen said.

"Bauer crashed right into you," Chris went on. "Didn't you see him coming? I yelled at you."

Everything came back to Eric: Bauer, Stoneface, the dream. Instinctively, he turned toward the street. Stoneface was still there. And this time Eric stared back, no longer feeling frightened, but confused. *Why are you looking at me? What is it?* he wanted to call.

Looking back to Chris, Eric said, "I remember now. I didn't see Bauer. I mean, I saw him. I had to see him. I just didn't react fast enough, I guess."

"I'll say! You just froze, staring out at the street like Stoneface had you spooked or something!"

"Hey, yeah! Look!" Bauer exclaimed. "Stoneface is there!"

"Maybe he's got Eric fingered for a stone person!" Josh laughed.

"Okay. Cut the wisecracks," Mr. Jensen said, helping Eric to his feet. "Chris, you stick close to him while he's getting changed, then walk with him to the nurse's office."

"I'm fine. Really," Eric insisted, forcing himself to stay standing. He looked cautiously toward the street again only to see Owen starting onto the field. Their eyes met, and Owen stopped walking. He smiled and nodded, as if to ask, "Are you all right?" Eric wanted to smile back, but the pain in his head was so intense that for a moment he thought he would pass out or throw up or both.

"Come on," Chris said. He took Eric by the arm and helped him toward the gym door.

"Hurt much?" Chris's voice broke the damp, heavy silence of the empty locker room.

Eric sat on a bench, holding his head in his hands. "I'm okay," he said, even though it hurt just to speak. "Chris?"

"Yeah?"

"What did Josh mean when he said maybe Stoneface has me fingered for a stone person?"

"It's just this stupid game we used to play."

"What game?"

Chris laughed. "It was like freeze tag, except whoever was 'It' was Stoneface, and if you were tagged, you were turned into a stone person. Hey, I don't understand how you couldn't see Bauer coming?"

Eric didn't answer. He was thinking about the Stoneface game.

Chris touched his shoulder. "Hey, Eric—Eric, you okay?"

Eric looked up.

"You feel okay? You want me to get Mr. Jensen or something?"

"No. I'm okay. Chris, I've got to tell you something . . . But you have to swear you won't tell Bauer or anyone."

"Well, sure."

"It's going to sound crazy."

"So?" Chris grinned, and sat down next to him.

"The reason I didn't see Bauer . . ."

"Yeah?"

"It *was* because of Stoneface."

"What do you mean?"

"When I saw him standing there, my mind went blank. All I could think of was him—he was watching me, Chris. I know he was. He watches me all the time. Well, maybe not all the time, but whenever I see him in town, he stares at me like he did that day you and I met him. Sometimes he's on his bike and sometimes he's driving that beat-up old jeep. And the other day, when I took Buddy to the playground, he was there, watching me. I know it!"

Chris was silent for a moment. "Look, Eric. You hit your head pretty hard. You blacked out. And what Josh said about the stone people—well, it was just a dumb game . . ."

"It's not what Josh said! And it's not the game! And it's not my head! I know what I know, Chris. And I know Stoneface *is* watching me, following me!"

"Okay, okay. So say he is. Let's just suppose it's true. It's still nothing to worry about. Owen may be a little weird, but he'd never do anything to hurt you. You don't have to be afraid of him. Take my word for it. My father's known him for years."

Eric sighed. "That's what's so weird. I'm not really scared. Sometimes I am, but it's more like—well—sometimes I get the feeling he wants to talk to me or be my friend."

Chris laughed good-naturedly. "Now I know it's your head. Stoneface is a hermit. He's lived alone on his mountain for I guess twenty-five years. Hermits don't want friends. If they did, they wouldn't be hermits. Come on, I've got to take you to the nurse."

"Chris, it's not in my mind—is it? I mean, you did see Stoneface out there today?"

"Sure. Bauer did. Jensen did. Everybody did. But I don't know what that proves . . ."

"Me either. But you know what I've been thinking?"

"No."

"Maybe I should go out to Stoneface Mountain."

"What?"

"Maybe I should—"

"I heard you. But . . . It's a real long bike ride, Eric. Stoneface Mountain is way out Route 80, near the reservoir. And then you have to go a mile on this narrow dirt road. And then you have to hike up the mountain . . ."

"You don't have to come with me."

"Hey, it's not that . . ."

"I'm really not telling you because I want you to come. I mean, I understand if you don't."

"No, it's okay," Chris insisted. He stood up.

"I'm not sure I want you to, Chris. I think I have to go alone."

"Have to?"

"Want to. Same difference."

"I don't get you."

"Maybe it's the bump on my head," Eric said. But he knew that even before the soccer game he'd felt himself drawn to this man, Owen Cassell. Drawn—connected . . . How could he explain that to Chris? How could he expect Chris to understand when he didn't understand it himself?

Ξ

COULDN'T SLEEP. WENT FOR A BIKE RIDE—*Eric.*

He left the note on the pad underneath the phone where all the comings and goings of the Nicholson family were recorded, and set out along Route 80 for Stoneface Mountain early the next Saturday morning. The road was winding and hilly, leading through the sparsely populated end of town. After he passed the development where Bauer lived, he pedaled for what seemed like miles before he came to another small group of houses. A little farther on was a big white house standing close to the road. After that, he saw only infrequent driveways to indicate anything was up in the woods besides trees.

At the end of Route 80, the road around the reservoir split off in two directions. To the left it was two laned and paved. To the right it was narrow and unpaved. Eric turned right. The road, which had turned to mud with the early spring thaws, had frozen overnight into a slippery, rutted, bumpy mess. Steering the bike soon became an impossibility. Chris's estimated mile from Route 80 to the road up Stoneface Mountain seemed more like ten to Eric as he pushed the bike against the wind blowing off the reservoir, whipping cold, damp air through his lightweight jacket.

He stopped to look out over the reservoir. There wasn't much to see—a thick, heavy fog hid everything except the little white caps rolling across the water. It was strange; there'd been no fog on Route 80 and now it stretched endlessly before him. A strong gust of wind made him shiver. *I've got to be crazy coming here alone,* he thought. *Maybe I should have come with Chris . . .* But he kept on.

When he finally reached the road up the mountain, he dropped his bike in the bushes. The road had been paved at one time, for there were areas of blacktop alternating with larger areas of dirt. Jeep tracks were evident in the frozen mud, and Eric knew he was in the right place. He started up. Trees and brush were gradually reclaiming more and more of the neglected road; it was wider in some parts then others. Melting snow was running off the mountain in such wide gullies there was hardly room enough for one car to pass. *No wonder Stoneface drives a jeep*, Eric thought.

Suddenly the road curved sharply, twisting even deeper into the black woods. Eric followed slowly, fighting his rising fear of being swallowed up by the darkness at any moment. He thought of Chris and the others coming up on Halloween—*or any other night for that matter. That took guts. But at least they came together. I've got to be crazy coming up here alone*, he reminded himself again, but he had no thoughts of turning back now. The woods, the road and the mountain seemed to urge him on: the road curving and twisting into the blackness of the woods, dissolving into the huge mass of the mountain. The unknown was all about him, threatening, and exciting.

A strong wind began blowing. The tall, thin trees swayed, moaned and cracked around him. He looked up. If there had been any sun, it was gone now. All he could see were brown leafless branches against a gray, threatening sky. *Maybe it's going to rain or snow, an early spring snow. Well, they never last long*. He wrapped his arms around himself to keep warm, and quickened his pace. His mother was always accusing him of pushing the seasons—wearing his spring jacket before spring was really here and his winter jacket when it was still Indian summer. *Maybe next time I'll listen to her.* He laughed. He laughed long and loud and the sound of his voice was reassuring.

When the wind died down, Eric could hear a distinct tapping. He'd heard it before but thought the wind was making it. Tap, tap, pause. *No, definitely not the wind.* Tap, tap, pause. His heart skipped a beat. Tap, tap, pause. He was near Stoneface's house. He knew it. He halted for a moment to take a deep breath and calm the pounding of his heart. When he began again, his long strides quickly became a fast walk.

Tap, tap, pause. Tap, tap, pause. It grew louder; and he began to run, stopping when the sky opened ahead of him—the trees suddenly ended and a meadow began. He ducked off the road and into the woods, making his way slowly, cautiously to the edge of the trees, then stopped again: tap, tap, pause—tap, tap, pause . . . It was the sound of the hammer against the chisel, the sound of Stoneface at his work.

A meadow of brown grass separated the forest from Stoneface's house—if it could be called a house. It was more than a house. It was a place, an experience, a powerful vision, breathtaking in its beauty and terrible in its destruction. In the middle of the meadow were the burnt remains of a house lying in charred heaps in a circle around a neatly laid out garden where several stone statues stood. It was clear the house had burned down years ago—not a wall or beam was left standing and the rubble was weathered as though it had long withstood the rain, the snow and the sun. In many places grass and small bushes had grown through it, nourished by the ashes and the decay. Like the road, the dead house was being reclaimed by nature.

About a hundred feet away was a cabin, crudely built out of partially burned wood, and timber cut from the forest. It was patched in places with large pieces of stiff, splitting black tar paper. Two odd windows were covered with plastic for winter protection, and a black stovepipe chimney spouting smoke stuck out from the slanted roof. A large woodpile was stacked neatly outside the door.

Eric quickly took in what he saw before his eyes rested on Owen, standing inside the garden amidst masses of white snowdrops and purple crocuses that drifted in waves about four stone statues. He was standing with his back to Eric, chipping away at a fifth, unfinished piece of marble. Tap, tap, pause. Tap, tap, pause. Eric became absorbed in watching him work, listening to the rhythmic beat of the hammer against the chisel, waiting for more and more of the hard, lifeless rock to fall away from the figure. Yet gradually his attention was drawn to the finished sculptures—it seemed impossible that they, too, had once been nothing but formless rock. For now they had a life force unlike anything else on the windswept mountain. Within the world of the burned-out house, the primitive shack, the brown grass, leafless bushes and barren trees, these statues seemed alive.

What did Chris call them? Stone people. Eric smiled to himself. "Stone people," he whispered softly.

He noticed the old stone woman first. Her dull, gray form had been left rough in places, making her seem gnarled and wrought in pain. Her head was bent, her face hidden, but her ancient arms reached toward the sky, her swollen fingers stretching, stretching even as Eric watched her. She was alive in her misery. Eric felt it as surely as if she had been screaming it to him; and he turned quickly from her.

A few feet away was the naked woman, the one on whom Arnold must have spray-painted his name. Her back was turned away from Eric and he wondered if "Arnold" was still written across her. He hoped it wasn't. She was beautiful, too beautiful. Eric stared at her for a long time, mesmerized by the white flowing body and hair, her smile and her eyes. She was looking in his direction . . . She was looking at him. Her smile was so lovely. He smiled back. He couldn't help it. There was something about her, so warm, so real—he needed to run to her and touch her, to make sure her skin wasn't soft and warm. He wanted to call to her to be certain she couldn't hear him. Her smile began to broaden, her eyes began to close, and her arms that fell so easily at her side moved ever so slightly. Had she seen him after all? Was she beckoning him?

He blinked his eyes, and when he looked again she stood as she had when he first saw her, as she would stand, look and smile forever. And that seemed unfair. He wanted her to be alive. He wanted her to see him.

Not far from her was a young marble boy crouching on the ground, his face turned down, his fingers curved, ready to pick up the insect or rock or whatever was lying before him on the ground. His bare toes were curled as though he were squishing them in the mud. At any moment, Eric expected the boy to leap up and shout, "Look! See what I've found!" And in between his fingers he would be holding a worm or a butterfly, and as he jumped, his thick dark hair would fly through the air . . .

Eric had to laugh. The boy's hair, like the rest of him, was white, marble white. But for some reason Eric knew it was meant to be dark brown, almost black, straight hair . . . *like mine*, he thought, running his hand over his hair, then turned uneasily away.

The last figure in the group was an old man who was separated from the others not only by distance but by feeling. He seemed dead—really dead, as though he had once been alive but had died. His hollow eyes stared blankly ahead of him; his face was expressionless; and his lifeless body seemed to draw its support from a roughly hewn cane. His stone gray clothes hung loosely as though the stone body had no flesh. Eric wondered why the old man was in the garden. He seemed less alive, less finished than even the fifth figure in the group, the unfinished one.

Eric was sure this figure would be a young boy, older than the crouching boy, but not full-grown. The muscles in his long, sleek legs and body were just developing. The legs were bent and taut as though the boy were running. The figure reminded Eric of himself, or of his friends. *I bet he's going to be my age*, he decided, trying to imagine what the unfinished boy would finally look like. *Will he be smiling like the woman? Will his hair be dark and straight like the crouching boy's? Will he be anything like me?* The idea shocked him. *Of course he won't! Why should he be? Come on, Eric! You're fourteen years old, for God's sake, not some crazy little kid!* He forced his attention away from the stone people's garden.

There must have been thirty or forty pieces of sculpture scattered beyond it throughout the meadow. Some were only heads, others bodies without heads. Still others were unfinished like the boy; but unlike the boy, Eric sensed these would remain unfinished, trapped forever in their slabs of cold rock. They seemed lost and forgotten, as though Stoneface had banished them to the other side of the circle of burnt rubble, outside the life-giving garden; and here they would remain until the meadow swallowed them up.

Eric didn't know how long he stood looking at the stone people. The rhythmic tapping lulled him, making him forget the cold and the strangeness of the place, making him forget he was spying; and he began to edge closer to the garden. It was fascinating to watch Stoneface work. He concentrated all his attention on the surface of the stone, constantly varying the angle of his tools, almost automatically raising his hand again and again to hit the butt of the chisel with the hammer. His movements were so swift, so continuous, that his arms and hands seemed independent of the rest of his body. They were one with the tools instead, which were one with the stone.

The sound of a voice stopped Eric suddenly. The voice was muted, but he knew it was Owen Cassell's. Stoneface's. It had to be. Nobody else was alive in the meadow besides him. As Owen dropped his tools on a nearby box and turned toward the other stone people, Eric fell instantly to the ground, hoping the winter grass would hide him. He lay as flat as he could, his head pressed to the earth, his heart pounding louder and louder until he was sure its beating would give him away.

"Well, my darling, how do you think he's coming?" Owen's voice boomed across the meadow. There were a few moments of silence and he began again. "I'm glad you think so. I'm sure I've got him this time. It's Michael without a doubt."

Eric raised his head just a little to make sure another human being hadn't appeared. Owen was still alone, examining the unfinished boy. Turning to the smiling woman, he went on. "What do you mean there's too much tension in the right leg?" he demanded, clearly annoyed. "The right leg's perfect. Just the right amount of tension. He's not an olympic runner—even though that's what you'd like me to make him. He's a boy, just a boy in youthful pursuit—playing soccer, if you will . . ."

Soccer—the word made Eric shudder. *It could be a coincidence! It could!*

Owen went on impatiently. "He's Michael for God's sake—and Michael's what he'll be forever! I won't glorify him. Not for you. Not for anyone. He'll be as I see him or not at all. And if you don't like it, then I'm sorry. I've given in to you enough times; but this is something on which I'm standing firm."

Owen turned from the stone woman as if there were nothing more to say.

The stone woman's mouth turned down slightly in a frown—or so it seemed to Eric. *Stop it!* he pleaded to her, flattening his head against the cold ground.

"Nothing more, Celia! My decision is final. I've waited too long. This boy is mine. I've found him!" Owen's voice exploded in Eric's ears.

What boy? he wanted to shout out. *What boy did you find, you crazy weirdo? What boy is yours? Because it better not be me. It better not be me!*

Tap, tap, pause. Tap, tap, pause. Owen was working again on the unfinished boy. The beat maddened Eric now, and he was overwhelmed by a desperate urge to get away from this place, from this man, Owen Cassell—Stoneface, from the stone woman and the unfinished stone boy. He began crawling slowly backwards across the meadow toward the woods.

"He's mine, Celia!" Owen shouted again.

"No, I'm not! I'm not!" Eric mumbled frantically. He knew he had lost all his control. He couldn't stay here a moment longer. He jumped up, not caring who or what saw him, and ran across the meadow, through the woods to the road.

Tap, tap, pause. Tap, tap, pause. The sound followed him, threatening him, echoing all about him. He ran faster and faster until all he could hear was the echo of his footsteps in the black woods.

Ξ

Eric waited impatiently for Chris on the front porch. He needed Chris. He needed to tell him what he'd seen and heard on Stoneface Mountain. For some crazy reason he'd thought he could tell his parents—

Right away his father had become upset because he'd biked out to the reservoir. And then there was his sister, Kathy: "Oh, you mean Stoneface? You went out to see Stoneface? How could you, Eric? He's so creepy and dirty . . . Oh, Mom, you've seen him around town. Everyone has . . ."

Yes, his mother had seen Owen. "You don't mean that seedy looking character with long gray hair and a beard? I see him wandering up and down the aisles at the A&P. He never seems to know where he's going. What were you doing going out to his place, Eric?"

And Eric had tried to explain—something about the

stone people, and lots of kids going out to see Owen's place, and Chris, Josh, Arnold and Bauer on Halloween . . . But it hadn't made sense, not even to him.

Maybe I could have explained it better, he thought. *But still, they wouldn't have understood. They're so hung up on the way Owen looks. What's wrong with looking seedy? No, not seedy—different. Besides, I like the way he looks. I like it a lot . . . Maybe he looks strange around town, but not on the mountain. He fits on the mountain . . .* And he remembered Owen working, and talking to the stone woman, *like she was real. Boy, Mom and Dad would love that!* He laughed to himself. *I wonder if Chris knows Owen talks to the stone people? I wonder if he knows Owen thinks they're real? So what? I thought the stone woman was real, too. For a minute, I really did. And I'm not crazy.* He laughed again.

"What's so funny?"

Eric looked up. Chris was watching him.

"Huh? What?"

"Do you realize I've been standing here for at least thirty seconds? I called you from the street. Man, you're really off in another world."

"Am I ever!"

"So? How was it?"

Eric grinned. "Pretty fantastic!"

"Then you made it all the way up?"

"Of course! What did you think?"

"I figured you'd make it maybe to his road, and maybe even part way up, and then turn around."

"How could I turn around when I got that far?"

"Easy!"

"Not a chance. But let's talk in my room. I don't want my parents or Kathy hearing this."

"Well, you've got to admit it was creepy," Chris said as they started up the stairs.

"Shh . . ." was all Eric said until they were in his room with the door closed. Then he began, "Well, it was freaky at first. I mean, it's a weird place, there's no getting around that. The way everything grows wild, and all that burned-down stuff and then, whammo—right in the middle that garden with the stone people . . ."

"How about the woman? Isn't she something?"

Eric didn't answer. He barely heard Chris.

"I mean, does she have some body, or what?"

Eric looked up. "Do you realize he actually carved those stone people out of stone? He must have started with a huge rock or something and he *made* the stone people from it!"

"Yeah . . . So?"

"Can you imagine doing something like that? It's so incredible. I mean, think about it . . ."

Chris shrugged. "You know who that woman is? I mean, you're not going to believe this . . ."

"And he made them look so alive. I kept on having to tell myself—they're only stone."

"That woman is his wife. Do you believe that? Do you believe old Stoneface could ever have been married to someone who looked like that?"

"I thought you said he lived alone."

"He does. She died a long time ago."

"She'd be beautiful anyway. It wouldn't matter if she was naked or not."

"Yeah, but having her naked sure helps!"

Eric was laughing. "You're too much! Here we're talking about something that's probably really great art. Did you ever think of that?"

"Well, nobody said Owen isn't a good sculptor. Besides, what do you know about art?"

"Well . . ." Eric hesitated.

"Nothing. Right?"

"Well, maybe I don't. But I know what Owen did is something special. Because those stone people really look alive. And even you have to admit that. Nobody could make stone people like that unless they were really good."

"I'm not arguing with you. My father said that Owen used to be really well known and lots of people went up there to see his stuff. He's got some in museums."

"Chris?"

"Yeah."

"This is going to sound strange, but—I kept on wanting to reach out and touch the stone people. Did you ever feel like that?"

"About the woman? Sure!"

"Hey, come on! Be serious!"

"Okay, okay. I'm serious."

"Have you touched them?"

"Well, yeah."

"What do they feel like?"

Chris thought for a moment. "Really different from what you'd think. Not so much the old man and the old woman. They feel kind of what they look like—hard and gray. But the others look so soft and shiny. They're not of course. They're hard. They have to be!"

"Are they smooth?"

"Yeah! Almost silky. Smoother than a piece of wood when it's sanded until you can't sand it anymore. It's hard to explain because you know you're touching stone, but for some reason it doesn't feel like stone . . ."

"Does he let you touch them any time you want?"

"He used to. I doubt he'd let me within a hundred feet of them anymore."

"I wonder what the unfinished one will look like," Eric said. He hadn't meant to.

"Owen's never going to finish him! He stopped working on him years ago."

"But he has to!"

"What?"

"I mean—well, don't you ever wonder what he's going to look like?"

Chris shrugged. "I never thought about it."

"How do you know he's not going to finish him?"

"He told my father. That was supposed to be a statue of Owen's son, but he just can't finish it."

"Why not?"

"I guess it's too painful . . ." Chris shrugged again. "His son died. Didn't I tell you that?"

"No! When?"

"Gee, I guess about twenty, twenty-five years ago."

"How old was he?"

"Sixteen. Let's see, he was the same age as my father. And Dad's forty, so it must be twenty-four years."

Eric shivered suddenly. "How did he die?"

"In the fire. That's when Owen's wife died, too."

The image of the crouching stone boy flashed into Eric's mind. *That must be Owen's son, too, with the straight, dark hair.* "The house lying around the garden?" he asked. "Is that where they died?"

"Yeah, isn't that weird? He just left it lying there—just like it was after the fire. But that's Owen for you."

"But—but when did he start the statue of his son?"

"I don't know. It's been that way ever since I can remember."

"Chris—he was working on that statue yesterday. I saw him."

"So, maybe he's changed his mind."

"Don't you think it's strange that he's starting again *now?*"

"How do I know?"

"Don't you think there could be a connection?"

"A connection?"

"It fits together. I know it does!"

"What are you talking about?"

"The way Stoneface looks at me and follows me. And he was talking about the unfinished statue being a boy playing soccer . . ."

"You talked to Stoneface?"

"No! I didn't talk to him."

"Then who was he talking to?"

Eric felt lost for an explanation. He didn't want to tell Chris about Owen's talking to the stone people. It would only give Chris more to laugh about. After a moment, he said, "He was talking to himself, I guess. Something about the statue being a kid playing soccer . . . it just set my mind going."

"I get it—because you were playing soccer the other day?"

"Yeah. Right."

"It's just a coincidence."

"I'm not so sure."

"I am."

"But he doesn't stare at *you!*" Eric cried suddenly, frantically.

"You're going too far, Eric." Chris sighed. "I'm beginning to wish I'd gone with you."

Eric looked away, feeling confused and a little frightened. *Maybe Chris is right. I'm going too far, I really am . . .*

"Eric . . ."

The stone boy has nothing to do with me. Stoneface has nothing to do with me . . .

"Eric! Hey, Eric!" Chris took him by the shoulder. "Are you okay?"

"Yeah, I'm fine."

"You're not acting fine. You haven't been acting fine since you hit your head."

"Look, I just made up my mind. This whole thing with Stoneface and the stone people is crazy. I mean, you're right. The guy's a fruitcake, that's all. And I'm just going to forget about him."

"Are you serious?"

"I said I was! Now let's forget about it!"

All week Eric tried to forget the stone people. He tried to convince himself Chris was right. He tried to stop daydreaming about them, but he couldn't—the stone people had a way of creeping into his thoughts when he least expected them. He knew he had to see them again, if only to touch them once.

And he knew he had to tell Chris he was going. That was important. He wasn't sure why, because he didn't want Chris to come with him. He only wanted Chris to know.

—

"You're not really going to record that song again!" Eric shrieked as Chris flipped over the tape.

"I have another whole side just waiting for some music!"

"But you've already got it at least four times on one side."

"Four and a half, to be exact!" Chris grinned. And he lifted the needle to start the record again.

"No!" Eric cried out, jumping to his feet, pushing Chris away from the stereo. "I can't stand it! I can't stand hearing that song one more time!" he shouted, quickly ejecting the tape and holding it high in the air.

"Give it to me!"

"As a favor to me! Please! No more!" Eric begged as Chris tackled him.

"But it's the greatest song I've ever heard. Even you said so."

"Was! You've ruined it forever. It's the only thing you've been playing for the past week!"

"I can't help it! It's haunting me. It's driving me crazy! It's in my thoughts every waking and sleeping moment!" Chris said dramatically, grabbing the tape from Eric,

Eric was laughing too hard to stop Chris. And as the music started again, a pillow landed in his face.

"Cover your ears. That way you won't hear it!" Chris said.

"For fifteen minutes?"

"Okay. I'll tape it through the amp—but only for you."

"Thanks. You're a real pal. For that, I'll let you in on a secret—I'm going back to Stoneface tomorrow!"

"Why?"

"The same reason you're taping that song on both sides of a thirty-minute tape."

"What?"

"I can't stop thinking about that place and those stone people. And maybe Stoneface won't be there and maybe I can touch them. Or maybe he's done more work on that statue of his son and I can see . . ." He hesitated.

"See what?"

"I'm not sure."

"I thought you said this whole thing is crazy? That you were going to forget about it?"

Eric grinned. "I tried."

"I'm coming with you."

"No."

"Why not?"

"Look, it's nothing personal, Chris. I just want to go alone."

"Thanks a lot. What am I supposed to do all Saturday morning?"

"Listen to your tape!"

Chris turned from him and switched on the speakers, turning up the music full blast.

Ξ

Eric felt himself smiling as he stood at the edge of the meadow watching the early morning sun sparkling off the white marble bodies. Scanning the meadow for Owen, he marvelled at the change in the place in one short week. Spring had definitely arrived, and he thought he had never seen it look so beautiful as it did on Stoneface Mountain. Many of the white snowdrops in the garden had given way to tiny coral bells, and here and there patches of green were springing up. The trees and bushes were bursting with new buds, and the birds encircled the meadow in an unending chorus. Everything looked clean and alive in the soft morning light. Eric felt spring had come to the mountain only for him, as though the stone people had been expecting him, and this morning was their welcome.

Once he felt certain Owen was nowhere about, he began running across the meadow, faster and faster, jumping effortlessly through the ruins of the burned-out house and into the garden, his eyes moving constantly between the smiling woman and the unfinished boy. The woman was closer and he stopped in front of her. As he lifted his hand to touch her, his heart began pounding. He paused only inches away—so close and yet afraid to make contact, afraid of the cold, hard touch of the marble, afraid of the moment which would prove her only stone.

"Go ahead. Touch her," came a deep, soft voice.

Eric spun around. "I—I'm sorry . . ."

Owen smiled. "Somehow I thought you'd be back today."

"Back?"

Owen nodded.

"Then you saw me last week?"

"Yes."

"I'm sorry . . ."

"There's no need to be. I'm glad you're here. Do you like them?" Owen extended his hand toward the statues.

"The stone people?"

"Stone people? Yes. I suppose they are stone people, aren't they?"

"I didn't mean anything bad."

"Of course not. I didn't think you did. The name is so right. Absolutely correct. They are stone and they are people. I've just never put the thoughts together quite like that. But before I introduce you, I want to ask you—I was wondering how your head is?"

"My head?"

"I was passing by your school when you were playing soccer. I saw you go down."

"Oh, that—it was nothing."

"For a moment I thought you were hurt. I wanted to help, but then I saw your friends had you on your feet."

"I think I blacked out."

"Have you seen a doctor?"

"No. I'm okay."

"You have to be careful about things like that. Does your family have a doctor in town? Chris said you just moved in. I can give you the name of mine."

"No, thanks. We already have a doctor. My mother worries about things like that."

"Then why didn't she take you when you fell?"

"I forgot to tell her about it."

"Maybe you ought to now." He rubbed his hand over Eric's scalp. His touch was light and gentle. "There. Right there. I can still feel the bump."

"It's all right. I don't even think about it anymore," he assured Owen, feeling himself relaxing, drifting, being caught up as he had been that first day in the experience of this man, Stoneface, Owen, the creator of the stone people, of the unfinished boy . . . *Who is the unfinished boy?* Eric was desperate to ask. *Why is he playing soccer? Does he have anything to do with me? Or is he really just your son?*

Owen took his hand away and smiled.

Eric smiled back.

"It's incredible," Owen said.

"What?"

"The resemblance—when you smile. It's Michael. You remind me of him in so many ways, Eric."

"Who's Michael?"

"My son . . ."

Eric felt his body go numb, but before he could say anything, Owen exclaimed, "Oh! I've completely forgotten—I left the coffee perking away and some sausages cooking. I can smell them from here. The sausages must be burnt to a crisp by now! Are you hungry?"

"I don't know . . ." Eric hesitated.

Owen laughed. "Not for the burnt sausages! I promise you better fare than that! I can whip up new sausages and eggs in no time. Are you hungry?"

"I can always eat."

"Good then."

Eric had to walk quickly to keep up with Owen's long, easy strides. "I'm afraid we might be attacked by the smoke!" Owen exclaimed as he threw open the door. The sharp odor of burning fat poured out, and Owen charged in, grumbling to himself as he grabbed the frying pan from the stove and dumped it into the sink.

Turning to Eric, he said, "Well, come in! Come in! And excuse the mess. I'm not used to guests."

Eric looked around. The cabin was littered with books, papers, stacks of newspapers and unwashed dishes and cups. A sleeping bag lay rumpled on a cot and a pile of clothes was on the floor next to it. Smoke was still floating between the sink and the wood-burning stove.

"It reminds me of my room!"

"That's what I hoped you'd say. Just take the junk off that chair and pull both chairs near the stove while I clean up this mess. I'm really quite a good cook—although I suppose I'll never be able to convince you of that. Do you drink coffee? I think I might have some tea someplace but no juice, I'm afraid."

"Coffee is fine," Eric insisted, even though the only thing he liked about it was the smell of it brewing.

Owen started to scrub the frying pan. Eric dragged Owen's chair closer to the stove, then picked up the pile of papers from the only other chair. As he did, he noticed the paper on top. It was filled with sketches of Eric, his face and head from different angles. He thumbed through the pile, pages and pages, and all of them drawings of him. In some he was standing in different poses, in others running. Still others were sketches of only his arms or legs, his hands, eyes, and even of his nose and mouth.

"What do you think of them?" Owen asked.

"I've never seen pictures like these before."

"They're not strictly pictures as a painter would do," Owen explained, coming to look at them with Eric. "They're exercises, studies of your body in its three dimensional form. I go from these to the stone. It's in the stone where I try to capture your life. These are merely mechanical. It's the step between you as my life model, and the stone."

"But why did you do all these pictures of me? Why do you look at me and follow me?"

Owen didn't seem surprised by the question. "Have I frightened you?"

"I don't know. Maybe a little."

"A lot, I think. But I didn't mean to, Eric. I promise you I didn't. I never realized you noticed me until the day at the soccer game, when you became so frightened."

"How do you know that?"

"I could tell by the look on your face."

"It's just that I didn't know what you wanted from me."

"I'm sorry. I suppose I should have explained from the very beginning. But you see, I only wanted to observe you, to use you as a model for the sculpture I'm doing of Michael."

"The unfinished stone boy?"

Owen nodded. "I haven't touched that sculpture for years. Since before you were born. Michael died when he was sixteen. His mother died with him. It was an accident, a fire. And, although I was able to recapture my wife in the stone, Michael always escaped me for some reason—until I saw you. Often after watching you in town, I'd come home and draw or go directly to the stone. A life model is what I've been missing all these years. I tried to do Michael from memory. I have no photos or even old drawings of him. They were all destroyed in the fire. But memory is no good. It falls short of reality and goes far beyond it at the same time. Sometimes I can't remember him at all. I sit for days and nothing of him comes to me. Other times I see him as an angel or a god. And I know that image comes from my love and my loss. But when I saw you—my heart almost stopped. It's not so much that you look exactly like Michael. The shape of the face is different and his cheekbones were much higher," Owen said, touching Eric's face as he spoke. "The eyes, of course. It's in your eyes I see him most. There's something about you, Eric. I can't put it into words. You are yourself and something of that self is so much like my son . . ."

Owen's smile, his touch, his rich deep voice, mesmerized Eric. He felt suspended and peaceful. He had been right about Owen after all. He wasn't the Stoneface

Chris had told about. He wasn't some crazy old guy. He was different from anyone Eric had ever met. *And he does want to be my friend,* he realized, wishing this moment and all these feelings could be frozen in time or somehow captured, held, wrapped in a box and stored like a secret treasure.

"I'd better get to that breakfast or we'll have to call it lunch," Owen said. "How do you like your eggs?"

"Scrambled."

"You any good at scrambling?"

"I think I can manage it!"

"Good. Look in the refrigerator. You'll find everything you need there. The bowl is on that shelf, and I'm afraid we'll have to wash some silverware—some dishes, too." He sighed, looking at the pile in the sink.

The business of cleaning up and making breakfast preoccupied Owen, and he spoke little as he worked. It wasn't until they sat down to eat that he relaxed. "Ah," he sighed, "food does wonders for me. Especially breakfast. It's my favorite meal."

"I never have breakfast like this, except maybe on weekends."

"You should. It sets you up for the day."

"There's always so much confusion in my house in the morning. Sometimes I'm just happy to get out on time!"

"Do you have brothers and sisters?"

"Unfortunately. Kathy. She's eleven. And Buddy. He's five."

"So you're the oldest?"

Eric nodded.

"You do an adequate job of scrambling eggs. Why not whip some up for yourself in the morning?"

"I don't know. Maybe . . ." He grinned. It seemed so silly to be talking about eating breakfast with someone like Owen. Silly and nice.

"Have you ever seen the face in the mountain?" Owen asked as he spread a thick layer of jam on his toast.

Eric shook his head.

Owen handed him the jam. "Here, try some. I make it myself."

"Really?"

"Grapes grow wild all over the mountain, so every September I make myself a supply of jam for the year." He watched Eric as he spread the jam on his toast, waiting eagerly for an opinion.

"Hmm. It's really good."

Owen smiled happily. "So, I was asking you about the face of the old man in the mountain. He's wonderful. Truly a wonder of nature, sculpted by the ice, the wind, rain and time. That's why the Indians named the mountain Stoneface. He's a rather grim, foreboding fellow, but I like him. You have to go across the reservoir to see him, or you can climb to him. It's an amazing experience to feel his life against your flesh."

"His life?"

Owen nodded. "The Indians felt he was a symbol of the sacredness of the mountain. There's a cave at the top, behind the face in the stone. According to Indian lore, the spirit of Stoneface dwells there. The Indians went to the cave to commune with the great powers of the unknown and the forces of nature. Chiefs went there to ask Stoneface for help in leading their people. Old people went there to die. The sick and injured would be brought to the cave when the medicine man's medicine failed. It is said

Stoneface knows when a person's time to die has come."

"You don't believe that?"

Owen thought for a moment, and said, "I believe this mountain has a soul of its own and all of us who experience it become a part of it. It leaves us changed, and we can never go back to where we were."

—

After breakfast they returned to the garden. "I want your opinion on Michael," Owen said as they crossed over the burnt rubble.

"My opinion?"

"Yes."

"But I don't know anything about sculpture."

Owen didn't respond. Extending his hand in a wide, sweeping motion toward the stone people, he smiled. "You haven't been properly introduced. I apologize. First, this is Celia," he said, touching the smiling woman. "Michael, age six." He pointed to the crouching boy. "And the old man—I call him Nothingness."

"Nothingness?"

"He's not reached death and he's given up on life. Death would be a blessing to the poor wretch. He merely exists, for eternity. Nothingness."

"And who is she?" Eric pointed to the old woman.

"She," Owen sighed, walking toward her. "She is my accuser and tormentor. She is Celia."

"But I thought she was Celia." Eric motioned toward the smiling woman.

"They are both Celia," was all he said, and turned to the unfinished boy. "But this, this boy—he is the culmination of my work and life. When I finish him—ah, when I finish him—do you know how long he's taken?"

Eric shook his head.

"Twenty years. Does he look any different from last week?"

"I don't know. It's hard to tell."

"But you like him?"

"Oh, yes!"

"Good. I've been working on him from sunup to sunset almost every day since you were last here. I think I was inspired knowing that you'd seen him, for the work has been going as it used to, as though the life within the stone is leading me, flawlessly. Do you understand?"

"I don't think so."

"Come here." Owen held out his hand for Eric's.

Eric didn't move.

"What's wrong?"

"Nothing."

"Then come and touch him. What are you afraid of?"

"I don't know," Eric whispered.

"You want to touch him, I know."

"I do. But . . ."

"But what?"

"I don't know."

"Eric, you have given him life. I can feel it pulsating through him again. It's as though he's struggling along with me to be born . . . As with the face in the mountain, you have to touch to understand."

Owen guided Eric's hand along the stone boy's body. The smooth stone had been warmed by the sunlight. Eric's hand moved across the gentle swells of muscles, encircling the stone boy's leg with his fingers. He felt the tautness of the chest. It wasn't soft and warm like a living boy. He couldn't feel the blood flowing through the veins or the steady movement of breathing or the beating of the heart. The stone boy showed no such signs of life; yet he was alive.

"Close your eyes and let your fingers send his image to your brain," Owen whispered.

Eric touched the statue as would a blind man, gingerly at first, groping, then as the touch became familiar and the image clearer in his brain, he let his entire hand rub the smooth, now warm stone, absorbing the stone boy into himself.

"It's so weird. I can almost feel him moving!" he exclaimed, shivering suddenly. Opening his eyes, he pulled his hand away. "It's so weird, Owen. I know it's just my eyes playing tricks on me—but he seems so real. Like last week—I thought Celia was smiling at me."

"It is no trick, my friend. You are experiencing the life within the stone as not many people do. It is a gift from the earth. You must treasure it."

Owen moved closer to the stone boy and ran his fingers slowly, lovingly over him. "Michael, Celia, these stone people, have been cut from the rock, the very essence of the earth. The same stroke with which I free their life from the rock has been used by stone carvers since the first human being carved a story on the inside of a cave. Little has changed. It is the most ancient of the arts. When I work I feel as though the tapping of my hammer against the chisel is an echo of the ancient stone carvers and all who followed them. Our work binds us together and drives us on. Sometimes I feel it is that unity which is the life within the stone calling me, guiding me. It began long before me and will survive long after I am gone. To touch the stone and feel the power of its being is to touch a force of life beyond our own—intensely alive yet free from death. A force, which for lack of a better word, I call eternity."

The sound of Owen's voice echoed about Eric, and as he watched Owen, he was afraid to move, wondering if this moment itself might not be eternity.

That spring and summer of Stoneface was a time unlike any Eric had known, a time seeming almost to swell from the earth with the green of spring and to burst above the tall summer grass with the clusters of brilliant pink and gold meadow flowers. It was a time of sun-warmed mountain mornings and sparkling white marble, of days filled with Owen's coffee and Owen's talk, mountain walks, and hours of watching Owen work, chipping away at the stone boy—tap, tap, pause . . . tap, tap, pause . . . the fine white marble dust floating into the air, covering Owen's face, beard, and the front of his shirt, making Eric laugh—promising to go on forever . . .

Midday on the Mountain

For eternity, Eric thought as he stood staring in disbelief across the snow-covered meadow: Owen wasn't there cutting the stone—he was nowhere in sight. Nobody was.

But the tapping—I was so sure I heard it. I was so sure . . . This cold must be doing something to my brain. How could I think Owen would be working today? He must be in the cabin. We'll have coffee like always. And sit by the stove and talk . . .

As Eric started toward the cabin, a strong gust of wind blew, swirling the snow about him, blinding him. And although his gloves and boots were soaked through and frozen, he felt strangely warmed, as if the wind were sweeping with it the five years since he and Owen met, since he and Owen and Chris had shared in that time of Stoneface Mountain—*even though it took me all summer to get Chris out here. And even though he thought I was totally out of my mind when I kept telling him what a great guy Owen was.*

Eric smiled, remembering Chris that summer. For a long time Chris was the only one who knew about Eric's friendship with Owen. His knowing never seemed to be a problem until that day he exploded—and Eric didn't know why.

That Summer

"HEY, CHRIS! WHAT ARE YOU DOING OUT HERE?" ERIC called when he realized it was Chris biking toward him along Route 80. It was a crazy day for Chris to ride out to the mountain—hot and sticky, maybe the hottest day of the summer so far. And Chris was pedaling furiously, his face and shirt dripping with sweat.

Chris didn't answer until they stopped, side by side. Then he burst out irritably, "I thought I'd meet you sooner! It's a real trek out here!"

Blaming Chris's bad humor on the heat, Eric laughed. "Especially when it's over ninety. Didn't you ever hear of heat stroke?"

"Didn't you ever hear of being on time? I've only been waiting for you for an hour and a half!"

"Look, I'm sorry. Owen's been teaching me how to carve in the stone. I guess I forgot the time. Hey, why don't we go for a swim right here, in the reservoir?"

Chris kicked his bike pedal angrily, and snapped, "It's illegal to swim in the reservoir."

"So? Who's going to see us? There's only Owen and Stoneface out here. Owen wouldn't tell and Stoneface can't!"

Chris kicked the pedal harder.

"You're really sore?" Eric said.

"Yeah. Big surprise! You're finally catching on!"

"I don't know what you want. I said I was sorry."

"Big deal, man. Big deal! So you're sorry! Like I have nothing better to do all afternoon than sit around and wait for you!"

"So don't wait. I never asked you to wait . . ."

"You never *asked* me to wait? That's a laugh. You remember the last thing you said last night? Huh? You remember? 'I'll see you around noon. Wait for me and we can go to the pool.' That's what you said! If you don't call that asking someone to wait, then I don't know what you call it!"

"What are you pushing this for?"

"You said you'd be at my house by noon!"

"So I said it. Big deal! Do I have to report to you when I'm going to be late? Are we bound in blood to go swimming together every afternoon?"

"But I suppose you're bound in blood to come out here and see Owen every day?" Chris shouted.

Chris's yelling and the accusing anger on his face exploded about Eric. Something in his brain snapped. His nerve endings felt on fire, as if the heat of the sun were being beamed directly on him. *What's going on here?* he screamed to himself. *Chris could have come to the mountain with me any time. What's he making a big deal over? What's going on here?* And then words began pouring from his mouth, thoughts he knew were untrue even as he spoke them; but he couldn't stop himself.

"So that's it! Now you're telling me when I can see Owen? I mean, who do you think you are? Jesus, man, I don't need this from you! I really don't. I don't need to go swimming with you. I don't need you riding out here to meet me . . ."

"Ha! You think I rode out here to *meet* you? Don't you think it's possible I was just riding out here for the ride? Or is this place sacred to you? To you and Owen maybe?"

"That's the stupidest excuse I ever heard! You don't ride out here once all summer and you pick the hottest day of the year and you tell me it's just a coincidence?" He laughed. "God, what a jerk!"

Pain twisted Chris's face, and without speaking, he sped off toward the reservoir.

As Eric watched him go, a strange panic overcame his anger, leaving an empty feeling in the pit of his stomach. He swerved his bike around and started toward the reservoir, shouting, "Hey, Chris! Wait up!"

Chris didn't even slow down, and Eric had to pedal fast to catch him. "Would you stop? Would you stop a minute?" Putting on a burst of speed, Eric jammed his bike into Chris's, making it zigzag out of control.

Chris jumped off so as not to fall, and letting the bike drop to the ground, he ran toward Eric. "What did you do that for?" he screamed.

"What do you think?"

"I don't know!"

"To stop you!" Eric grinned.

"I can stop on my own. When I want to!"

"Look, this is crazy—I don't want to fight . . ."

"Tell me about it!" Chris glared back grimly.

"Hey, come on . . ." Eric hesitated, feeling unsure of what to say. There was something about the way Chris looked standing there, so angry—and so miserable. "I'm sorry. I didn't mean what I said back there. Come on—we're friends . . ."

Chris shrugged. "That's what I thought."

"We are. The best."

Eric was puzzled. Chris always seemed to understand about Owen, about the mountain and Eric's time there. He'd never minded before—or never seemed to. Eric wasn't sure he could bear it if Chris minded, if somehow he had to choose between Owen and Chris. *Hey, everything's okay, isn't it?* he wanted to say. He wanted it to be true.

For a moment neither boy spoke, then Chris turned away and started toward the reservoir. Picking up a rock, he hurled it into the water.

Eric followed, throwing a rock after Chris's. "Yours went farther. Want to try again?"

Without answering, Chris picked up two rocks, and handed one to Eric, saying, "Ready. On your mark. Get set. Go!"

The rocks whizzed through the air, crossing paths and splashing into the water almost simultaneously.

"Ha! I won!" Eric exclaimed.

"No way! Mine went farther!"

"Are you kidding? The one way out there is mine!"

"Prove it!"

"Okay!" Eric laughed, pulling off his sneakers and shirt.

"What are you doing?"

"I'm going to get my rock. I know which is mine because it had a hole in it!" he shouted as he raced toward the water in his cutoffs.

"Hey, you're not supposed to swim in the reservoir!"

"I know! You told me!" Eric shouted as he dove in.

Chris kicked off his shoes and followed.

When they were out above their heads, Eric jumped on Chris's shoulders, forcing him under water. "If you don't promise to forget this whole stupid thing, I'll drown you!" he shouted.

"Not if I drown you first!" Chris laughed as he pushed himself out of the water, knocking Eric in.

"I'll race you to that island," Eric dared him, pointing to a barren cluster of rocks a couple of hundred yards away.

"You'll never make it!"

"You want to make a bet!"

"You're on!" Chris agreed, plunging ahead.

Breathless, the boys dragged themselves onto the rocky island a few minutes later. "It's a tie," Eric moaned, flopping flat on his back.

"No way," Chris gasped, collapsing beside him. "My hand touched the rock first."

"Okay, okay—you win!"

They lay side by side, breathing heavily as the heat from the rock's surface and the warmth from the midsummer sun cradled their bodies. *I can probably see Stoneface from here,* Eric thought, opening his eyes, but the sunlight sparkling off the water blinded him. *Well, I bet Stoneface can see me! "That's right. It's me and Chris out here, Stoneface. We swam all the way!"*

"Chris?"

"Yeah."

"Do you believe we made it?"

"The question is—can we make it back?"

"I don't want to think about that."

"Me either."

"The sun feels so good . . ."

"Hmmm . . ." Eric sighed. *The sun feels good . . .* But then life had been good for Eric lately—it was hard to believe summer was half-over. It felt so endless, one hot lazy day drifting slowly into the next, with no set schedule, no time to get up and go to bed. For the first time, his life seemed his own. Despite his mother's nagging and constant worrying, Eric was rarely at home. Most mornings he went to the mountain, and in the afternoons he met Chris, grabbing lunch and often dinner where they could, staying out until past eleven; and even then it seemed too early to go home. He knew sleep wouldn't come for hours. It never did on summer nights when the heat kept his brain awake, and he'd lie naked on the bed, trying to forget he had a sweltering body . . .

He always woke up refreshed, surprised he'd slept at all. Throwing on some clothes, he'd slip quietly out of the house before anyone else was up. Owen always had breakfast waiting. And as he rode his bike along the silent, empty streets, his house, the town, and the development where Bauer lived would fall behind him, and he'd feel himself slipping into the world of Stoneface Mountain.

Gradually Eric grew aware of the sun again. It was beginning to burn his skin. He was dripping with perspiration now; and he could almost feel the heat streaming off Chris's body. They were both sweating. The acrid odor seemed out of place on this smooth rock in the middle of the calm, clear reservoir. *God, the sun is hot. I wonder if Chris is as hot as me. I wonder if he wants to go for a swim . . .* But he didn't say anything. In a way, it felt good lying on the rock in the sun, not talking, close to Chris.

"Eric," Chris finally moaned, "I think I'm burning up."

"Me, too."

"Want to go back?"

"You?"

"I don't know. It's kind of nice out here." Chris sat up. "Besides, land looks awfully far away."

"We could stay here forever."

"Now there's a thought! Of course, food is a little scarce."

"True. But it's better than drowning!"

They laughed.

"This is crazy . . ." Eric said.

"What?"

"You and me fighting—what do we have to fight about?"

Chris stared silently across the reservoir at the mountain.

"I can't not go to Owen's," Eric went on.

"I never said that."

"Then what are you saying?"

"I don't know." Chris sighed. "I really don't. Before, when I started out, I just thought I'd meet you. I figured I'd meet you somewhere around Bauer's. But when I kept on riding and I didn't see you, I started getting madder and madder. And I kept on thinking this is crazy—it was like I was two people inside my head, you know. And one of the people was saying, 'So what if Eric's not back when he says? He's always late. Why don't you just turn around and go to the pool? He'll show up eventually.' And then there was this other person who was getting really mad at you and Owen. I mean, sometimes it bothers me that you go out to Owen's so much, but not really, not like it did when I was riding out here. It was like my brain was going to burst, and if it did, I only wished it would blow up all of Stoneface Mountain with it."

"And me and Owen, too?"

"You better believe it!"

"Why don't you come to the mountain with me sometime?"

"I don't know. Maybe."

"You won't."

"You never know!"

"Tomorrow?"

"Oh, sorry—I can't tomorrow!"

"Why?"

"Big plans."

"Sure . . ."

"You think I can't have big plans without you?"

"Like what?"

Chris grinned his silly, zany grin and said, "Well, you see, me and three beautiful girls . . ."

"Do I know any of them?"

"I'm sworn to secrecy."

"The question is—do *you* know any of them?"

"Ah—you're jealous. I can see it already!"

"Hey, Chris, let's us do something tomorrow, something different."

"And give up my three beautiful girls? I mean, you haven't heard my plans!"

"I'm serious. What's that place you were telling me about—where you dive off the cliffs?"

"Grosset Lake?"

"Yeah."

"It's an all-day trip. We'd have to leave early, before it's too hot."

"Sounds good to me."

"What about Owen?"

"I don't have to go every day. Besides, he's just about finished with the stone boy. He'd probably like it if I wasn't around to bug him."

Chris stopped his bike beside Eric. "I think we're lost."

"I told you that twenty minutes ago!"

"I was sure that last turnoff was right."

"We've made so many turnoffs you thought were right, I don't think we'll ever find our way home, much less to Grosset Lake!"

"We can't be that far off. I'm sure of it. I checked the map before we left."

"You should have brought the map."

Chris shrugged.

"Well? What do we do now?"

"We could have lunch." Chris grinned sheepishly.

"At ten o'clock in the morning?"

"Why not?"

"What'll we do for lunch, then?"

"I have two dollars. What about you?"

Eric reached into his pocket. "I've got a dollar and eighty-seven cents."

"That should get us lunch. There's a place near the lake."

"If we ever get to the lake."

"We will. But let's get off the road for a while. The sun is beginning to make me sick."

"Where are we going to go?"

"In there," Chris said, pointing to the nearby woods. "Ever been in a pine forest?"

"Not that I remember."

"Come on then," Chris said, dropping his bike by the side of the road.

It was dark and cool inside the forest. The ground was covered with a thick, soft layer of brown pine needles. They hadn't gone far when Chris sat down and began taking off his sneakers.

"What are you doing?"

"I remember once when we were on vacation in Maine—it was a long time ago, but we found a forest like this. And I have this memory of all of us—my mother and father and Frank and me—we were all walking around in this pine forest barefoot."

"Why not?" Eric said, pulling off his sneakers, too. He picked up some of the pine needles and let them fall through his fingers, then dug his toes into the ground. Underneath the needles the soil was rich, dark, cool and moist. Eric looked up for Chris, but he was gone, walking deeper into the forest. Tucking his sneakers and lunch under his arm, Eric scooped up some pine needles, and, sneaking up on Chris, he dumped the needles on Chris's head and ran off, crashing through the trees, not stopping until he heard Chris cursing as he cried out in pain. Eric turned to see Chris hopping on one foot, grasping the other foot in his hand. And Eric couldn't help laughing.

"Oh, it's real funny!" Chris screamed.

"Stub your toe?"

"Yeah! And it's bleeding!"

"That'll teach you to go barefoot!"

Chris dropped hold of his foot and charged after Eric.

Eric took off, dodging in and out of the trees, finally stopping to catch his breath, although he was winded more from laughing than running.

Chris was nowhere to be seen.

"Chris! Hey, Chris!"

"Over here!" Chris's voice sounded far away.

"Where?"

"Here!"

"That's a help!" Eric began walking in the direction of Chris's voice. "Where are you?" he called again.

"Here!" Chris finally appeared, soaking wet. "Come on. Look what I found!"

About fifty feet away the trees ended, opening onto a pond flooded with sunshine.

"It's pretty deep," Chris said. "And the bottom is muddy and disgusting; but there are some big fish down there. I don't know if they're catfish or what."

Eric stood at the edge, peering in. "It looks so slimy. You really went in there?"

"It's not so bad. It's not so good either, but it's not so bad!" And he shoved Eric.

Eric fell in, his sneakers, socks and lunch hurtling into the air, landing in the middle of the pond. He quickly retrieved his sneakers and socks, but his lunch was ruined. "I'll get you for this, Praeger!" he warned, throwing his sneakers onto the ground and dragging himself from the water.

"Okay! Okay—you can have half my lunch!"

"I might just take it all!"

"That I doubt!"

"Ha!" Eric laughed, pouncing on Chris's lunch, which was lying on the ground only a few feet away. Chris was on top of him instantly, trying to pry the bag loose. Eric wouldn't let go; and suddenly the bag ripped. Chris's sandwich, peach and cake went flying. The peach ended up bobbing in the pond, and as the sandwich hit the ground, the wrapping split and the ham, cheese and bread spilled into the dirt. Eric managed to get to the cake before Chris, and he took off around the pond, stuffing the cake into his mouth as he ran.

"Oh, God!" Eric moaned, finally collapsing on the ground. "That was good cake."

"What am I supposed to eat?" Chris demanded, but he was laughing when he dropped down next to Eric.

"I'll get you the peach when I get my strength back."

"Thanks a lot!"

"Hey, you know, this is kind of a nice place. It was almost worth getting lost to find it."

"I think I know where we made the wrong turn. I think we're only about ten minutes from Grosset Lake."

"Sure, sure."

"I mean it!"

Eric stretched out on the ground, relaxing in the sun. "Let's stay here a while," he said.

Chris got up and started for the water.

"Where are you going?"

"To get my peach. I don't trust you!"

Ξ

If Eric had thought about it, he would have realized something was wrong as soon as he reached the meadow the morning he returned to the mountain. It was cool and sunny, the kind of weather Owen loved. Eric expected to see him working on the stone boy or tending to the flower beds in the stone people garden. Instead Owen was in the cabin, hunched over his desk amid a mass of sketching paper. Dirty dishes and half-drunk cups of coffee were scattered around. Owen was so absorbed in what he was doing, he didn't hear Eric come in. Eric hadn't seen him working inside like this in weeks; but he was too excited about being back—he hadn't been to the mountain in five days—to wonder about it long. Walking quietly over to Owen, he tapped him on the shoulder.

Owen spun around, his look of surprise quickly turning to a smile. He reached out and grasped Eric's hand. "Well, well—it's good to see you, my friend!"

"It's good to be back!" Eric could feel himself grinning all over.

"Tell me—where have you been and what have you been doing? You haven't been ill, have you?"

"No. Chris and I got into this whole thing of biking out to Grosset Lake."

"Grosset Lake? You mean over in Phillipstown?"

Eric nodded.

"You biked out there and back for the past five days?"

"Yeah. I think we're insane."

"You must be exhausted. That's quite a ways to bike."

"I almost couldn't make it out here this morning."

"Then you sit down and rest and I'll make you breakfast. You haven't eaten, have you?"

"You know me!"

"Good, I'm starved, too."

"Owen, is the stone boy finished yet? Can we go out and see him first?"

Owen grew silent. His smile vanished.

"What's wrong?"

"There was a flaw in the stone," he said finally. "I've known about it—for weeks. But I thought if I were careful . . ."

"A flaw?"

"The stone cracked, right down the side of his face."

Eric felt sick, as if someone had just punched him in the stomach. "What?" It still didn't make sense.

"Come, I'll show you."

Eric stared in pained silence at the wounded stone boy. He looked as if someone had taken a knife and sliced off half his face. It seemed impossible. He had been so perfect, so beautiful . . . "When did it happen?"

"Three days ago."

"If only I had stopped by. I meant to . . ."

"There's nothing you could have done, Eric. There's nothing anyone could have done."

"But you can fix him. Right? That's what you were working on inside. You're going to fix him, aren't you, Owen?"

"There's nothing I can do now."

"But that's not fair. It's not fair!"

"Not fair . . ." Owen's voice softly echoed Eric's. "How many times have I thought life not fair . . . No, I'm afraid fairness is not very much to the point, my friend."

"But this is so stupid. So dumb! Why couldn't it have happened at the beginning? Then it wouldn't have mattered so much. Then maybe you could have just started all over."

"I still can. In fact, that's exactly what I intend to do."

"You mean a whole new stone boy?"

"Yes. I'll take everything I've learned from this one to make the new one even better. I've already started on the sketches."

Eric turned from Owen. He could feel his throat tightening and his eyes threatening to fill with tears. He couldn't imagine a new stone boy. He couldn't imagine anything better than this one.

Owen put his arm around Eric's shoulder. "I know it's hard for you to believe, but I promise you the new stone boy will be everything this one is. He's still alive for me. I can feel him. If he weren't, then all would truly be lost."

"But how do you know? How can you be so sure?"

Owen turned from Eric, staring silently at the mountain. Finally he said, "Remember the cave I told you about?"

"The Indian cave?"

"Yes. That's how I know. That's why I'm sure."

"I don't understand."

"It's impossible to explain. You have to see the cave to understand . . ."

The cave was hidden deep within the woods near the mountain top. The entrance was small, and Eric would easily have missed it if Owen hadn't been leading him. They had to crawl through it on their hands and knees. It was pitch black inside.

"Wait here," Owen said, quickly disappearing into the blackness. Then the sound of a match being struck, a flicker of light, and a torch on the side of the cave burst into flame. The cave became aglow with a soft yellow light.

"Come on in," Owen said.

Eric stood up. The cave was much bigger than he'd expected, the size of a small room. The walls were smooth and curved, as though they'd been wrought by hand. The floor was made of fine pebbles, so tiny they seemed almost like sand. In the far corner, opposite the torch, were two small mounds of rock. Other than that the cave was bare, majestic in its stark simplicity.

"It's a place of wonder," Owen said. He spoke softly. His voice sounded far away. "Of another world, another life. It's beyond us and yet transports us."

Eric reached up to touch the walls. He rubbed them with his hands. Their hardness surprised him. Their smooth, cold dampness made him shiver. In the light of the torch, the walls had appeared almost translucent, the cave boundless.

"Do you see why the Indians felt this was a sacred place?"

Eric nodded. He was afraid to speak. Owen's voice blended with, almost faded into, the sensation of the cave; but Eric feared his own would come out harsh and out of place no matter how softly he spoke.

Owen sat down, leaning against the cave wall. Eric sat opposite him, watching as the light danced across his face in flickering shadows, making Owen himself seem to fade in and out of existence.

It's the light, Eric thought, looking up at the flame. It flowed in warm colors throughout the cave, leaving nothing untouched, unchanged, making Eric feel airy, almost giddy, as though the weight of his body were gone. He felt as one with the strange unearthly light. *I have to tell Chris about this place*, he thought. *Maybe it will get him to the mountain.* And he closed his eyes. The light stayed with him, sifting slowly into his mind and body until he relaxed against the wall, drifted . . .

"I used to come here often; but I understood nothing." Owen spoke suddenly, his voice jarring Eric. "I was a tourist only, until the fire."

Eric opened his eyes. He wondered if Owen were speaking to someone else, for he was looking right past Eric, across the cave at the two mounds of stone.

"After the fire I came here to die," Owen went on. "I thought I was losing my mind. I'd seen the flames from the mountain top. It was nighttime, and in the light of the full moon, the flames seemed to reach the sky. By the time I got to the house, it was engulfed. I searched for Michael and Celia. I searched all night. The firemen finally told me they were dead. But I had eyes. Nothing was left. Only a smoldering heap . . .

"I couldn't believe it. I still can't. I like to think Celia and Michael never existed, except in my mind and in the stone where they will never suffer again—never know death. Perhaps that's why I can't mourn the stone boy. His life is eternal. It was there all these years. I simply couldn't touch it until I saw you. I've waited so long for him, you see. Twenty years. Another year won't matter. But then, after the fire, I didn't understand such things. I knew only that I had to die myself. I came here and lay for days, waiting for death. My mind was on fire. All I could think of was Celia and Michael, and each memory of them seemed like a thousand knives being thrust into me. A person can't live long with such pain. I knew my time had come, but I couldn't die. I thought the spirit of Stoneface was playing a cruel joke on me.

"One morning I woke up and the pain was so much

less, it seemed to have left me. I found myself thinking of the magnificent new piece of marble I'd just received. I'd helped cut it from the ground myself. Only two other people had ever touched it. And in my mind I began to see Celia in the marble. I tried to remember the texture and the lines of the stone and suddenly my hands were aching to touch it. I knew I had to live if only to give Celia life again. But it was years before I touched that piece of marble. First I did Nothingness. Then old Celia. I already had the young Michael. He was the only one of the old sculptures I left in the garden after the fire. Finally I did my beautiful Celia in the marble. And now I will do Michael again. Of that I am certain."

Then Owen was silent.

For a few moments the sounds of his voice and the memory of all he'd said continued to echo in Eric's mind until it became lost, along with everything else, in the streams of light flowing from the torch. He felt giddy once more; and he closed his eyes. The light stayed with him. He was drifting toward it now, the light growing more intense, swelling, rolling like waves up a sandy beach until he felt it overwhelming him, enveloping him in brilliant bands of red, orange and yellow. They swirled about him, catching him up, spinning him around as they whipped through the cave like a sun tornado. *This is fantastic!* he thought, feeling suddenly that he'd been here before. *But I haven't. Have I? Owen, did you bring me here before? But where is here? Where am I?*

He reached out to touch the walls, to make sure he was still in the cave. The cool wetness made him shiver; and as he did, the light exploded about him once again, grabbing him up and spinning him around with such force he feared he might be suddenly hurled loose, outside of the light, where everything was in darkness.

Owen? Are you still there? Can you see me?

Almost in answer to his call, Eric heard the sound of music—a tapping, like the distant ritual beating of drums from beneath the cave.

Owen? Is that you?

The music grew louder, building into an irresistible frenzy, overwhelming Eric as the light did. He felt himself moving with the frenetic tapping, swaying, spinning until he knew he had to go beyond the light.

He began to drift, to float again, into the cave itself, absorbed by its cool, wet blackness. Down, down, down he went, beyond the cave, deep within the earth. And as he did, the tapping grew louder—as if he were nearing its source.

He came to a place of polished whiteness: soft hills and deep valleys of sun-warmed marble stretched before him, turning suddenly sharp, angling into spearlike sculptures and stairlike cliffs, leading him as a wanderer to the edge of a sea of glittering diamonds. In the distance, tall mountains leveled off into planes of sheer ice whiteness, cascading suddenly into waterfalls, pouring, rushing into crystal ponds of sweet warm water where swimming was as effortless as walking. And all the while the music sounded, no longer the frenetic tapping, but a soft, steady, melodic pulse.

Owen? Are you here?

"Eric," Owen whispered, nudging him gently. "Eric, wake up."

Eric opened his eyes. Owen's face was so near, glowing

in the warm light of the torch. Eric wanted to reach out and touch him, to make sure he was real.

"You looked quite wonderful as you slept," Owen said. "The way I've tried to capture you in the stone."

"I was having the most incredible dream, about the light. I was dancing with it or something. And I went to this place where everything was white, like marble, except I was swimming. And there was music. I felt you were there, and the stone boy and Celia and all the stone people. We were together sort of, but I couldn't see any of you. It was really weird! How'd you ever find this place, Owen?"

Owen sat back on his heels, folding his arms in front of him. "The first time I came to the mountain, before I had any thoughts of living here, I came to find the cave. I didn't, not then, not for several years. It was Michael who found it, one spring. He was eight. We were having a picnic on the mountaintop, feeding a family of squirrels as we ate. After they'd eaten their fill, they began scurrying back and forth, storing what we gave them. Michael followed them until they disappeared down a crevice in some rocks. He climbed the rocks to try to look in, and as he did, some of the rocks moved. He slipped and fell. The rocks shifted and his foot became lodged in between them. When he cried for us to help, he heard the echo of his voice behind the rocks. The three of us began pulling at the rocks, and it didn't take long before we discovered it was an entrance to the cave. Either the Indians or a rock slide had closed it up. If my calculations are correct, Stoneface is carved on the far outside of that wall," he said, pointing beyond the two small mounds of stone. After a silence, he smiled and continued, "I've been thinking about driving up to Vermont next week, to a quarry where I've gotten all my marble. It occurred to me that if you could come with me and help pick it out—we could cut it from the ground together—then you'd be a part of the new stone boy from the very beginning."

"Could I really help cut the marble from the ground?"

"Yes, I'll teach you. Wally and I."

"Who's Wally?"

"Tom Wallace. Everyone calls him Wally. He's been running the quarry for years. Lives there. Probably knows more about marble quarrying than anyone I know. We'll make a trip out of it, maybe stay a couple of days."

"Did all the stone people come from there?"

"All the marble ones. There are some like old Celia and Nothingness who are made from granite, and some from limestone, but the stone boy, of course, will be marble. He must be from the quarry. Well, what do you think?"

"I think it's fantastic."

"Yes. Yes. So do I! We can camp out. Go fishing. Ever have fresh caught fish grilled over a fire?"

"Nope. I've never even been camping. My parents aren't too big on the outdoors."

"We'll need some gear like a tent and sleeping bags. But we can go shopping together. It'll be fun. Providing of course, that your parents agree."

Eric felt all the excitement drain from him. His parents. He'd forgotten about them.

"You think they won't approve?" Owen asked.

"They better."

As the two of them walked down the mountain, Owen talked excitedly about the trip and the quarry, but Eric wasn't really listening. His mind was on other things: caves, quarries, stone people, Owen, the mountain—and how he could ever explain them to his parents . . .

Ξ

"It's supposed to be cooler tonight," Mrs. Nicholson said, closing her book and looking toward Eric.

"Hmm," Eric agreed. "It's nice out now."

After a silence, his mother asked, "Do you have something on your mind, Eric?"

"Who me?"

"I don't see another Eric here!" Mr. Nicholson laughed.

"You've been so quiet all evening. You only picked at your dinner. And now you're sitting in the living room with us when you're usually out with Chris. Did something happen between you two?"

"What? Oh . . . no." Suddenly he felt like forgetting the whole trip. *I'll just tell Owen, "No. My parents said no—just like I knew they would."*

"Eric?" His father's voice surprised him. "Did something happen to your bike?"

"No! Why?"

"Obviously you have something to tell us. Have you gotten into some sort of trouble?"

"Can't I have something to talk about without it costing something or being something wrong? Can't I just want to talk?"

"You could. But you usually don't . . ."

"Okay! If that's your attitude, then never mind!" Eric said angrily.

Mrs. Nicholson grabbed hold of his hand to keep him from leaving the room. "Your father was only joking. It might not be the best time to joke—but we've been concerned about you all evening. We know when something's bothering you."

Eric slumped down on the couch. "I don't see much point in bringing it up. I know you're going to say no anyway."

"You never know . . ."

Eric took a deep breath. "Remember I told you about Owen, the sculptor who lives on Stoneface Mountain?"

His mother nodded hesitantly.

"That character with the long hair?" his father asked. "Stoneface, I think Kathy called him."

Eric felt his stomach tighten, but he went on as calmly as he could. "Well, see—I've sort of gotten to know him. I mean, we're friends . . ."

Mr. Nicholson folded his paper and leaned forward.

"Now wait a minute, Dad. I know what you're thinking because of all that junk Kathy said. But if you'll just give me a chance—see, it's not true. None of it! Owen's very different once you get to know him. He's really terrific. He's teaching me how to carve in the stone. And he's used me for a model . . ."

"Hold on," Mr. Nicholson interrupted. "How long has this been going on?"

"I don't know. A while . . ."

"A few days? A few weeks? A few months?"

"A few months."

"You've been modeling for some character who lives

like a hermit miles from nowhere for a few *months* and you don't think that's important enough to tell us about before this!"

"I don't *model* for him, Dad. It's nothing like that . . ."

"Then what is it like?"

Eric was beginning to shake inside. "We're friends," he tried to say calmly. "We go for walks. We talk about art and nature."

"Art and nature?"

"Yes!"

"For God's sake, Eric—what do you know about art and nature?"

"What do you mean, Dad?"

"Take it easy, Lou," Mrs. Nicholson said. "All your father means, Eric, is that it's somewhat strange for an old man who's lived by himself for years to suddenly take a liking to a fourteen-year-old boy."

"But there's nothing strange about it, Mom!"

"Then why did you keep it from us, Eric?" his father demanded.

"I'm telling you now."

"Months after the fact!"

"I didn't tell you because I knew you'd react like this, because anyone who doesn't shave and wear perfectly pressed pants is seedy. Isn't that what you called Owen, Mom? Seedy? You've seen him a few times in the supermarket and zing—he's a seedy guy. Right? Like that's the worst thing in the world? Like anyone who isn't totally straight looking is bad news? Anything you don't agree with one hundred percent is bad news! Never mind what I think about him or what I feel. Right?"

There was a silence. Mrs. Nicholson sighed deeply and

said, "Believe me, Eric. Nothing's going to be resolved if you carry on like this. When I called the man seedy, I was merely making a casual observation. I had no idea he had any bearing on my life. But now, from what you're telling us, he does."

"*My* life, Mom—not yours!"

"Through you he has something to do with me, then. That's not what's important . . ."

"It is! That's the most important thing! Because if he's my friend and not yours then I should have the right to make my own decisions . . ."

"Oh, for God's sake, Eric—we're not talking about a school friend. If we were, the problem would never have come up!" Mr. Nicholson cried angrily. "We're talking about a fourteen-year-old boy and some old, *seedy*-looking character who's got a reputation for being strange. Now I'm assuming you've got more on your mind than just telling us you've made friends with this man. How did this whole 'friendship' get started in the first place?"

"I was with Chris one day, and we met Owen. But Chris's father knows him . . ."

"How well?" Mrs. Nicholson asked.

"I don't know exactly. Mr. Praeger went to school with Owen's son."

"Is Chris in on this friendship with Owen, too?"

Eric sighed. "Not exactly."

"So it's just you and the sculptor?"

"Yes, Dad."

"Okay. Go ahead. I just want to get the picture clear in my head."

"Anyway, Owen and I got to talking. He said I reminded him of his son and he'd been trying to do a sculpture of his son since his son died . . ."

"When was that?" Mrs. Nicholson asked.

"Twenty-four years ago."

"How old was his son?"

"Sixteen. There was a fire. The whole house burned down. Owen's son and his wife died."

"Oh, my God! The poor man . . ."

"Wait a minute. Don't go feeling sorry for him right away, Laura. I want to get Eric's story. Okay?" And turning to Eric his father asked, "So Owen's been trying to do this sculpture for twenty-four years and he can't?"

Eric nodded. "He couldn't because he needed to sculpt from life . . ."

"And you're the life model?"

"Well, yeah, Dad—but it's not . . ."

"It's not what, Eric? That's the screwiest story I've ever heard! I suppose if somebody told you you looked like a movie star and he had a screen test set up for you in Hollywood, you'd fly out there without telling us!"

"No, Dad! I wouldn't. This isn't the same thing. You don't even know Owen!"

"I know enough!"

"Why didn't you tell us about Owen before?" Mrs. Nicholson asked.

"I did. I tried to . . ."

"You casually mentioned this man to us—but you never led us to believe you had a whole—friendship—with him."

Eric sighed and leaned back on the couch. "Look, he's a very nice person. I've never met anyone like Owen. We talk and talk and he never makes me feel like a kid. It's just like being friends with anyone else except better, in a way. He just likes me, Mom—and I like him. I don't see what's wrong with that. It's interesting, different. He has this whole idea about life and nature and the earth and the stone . . ." Eric tried to explain, but he felt so confused, helpless and angry. "I want you to understand about Owen. I really do. But you're not listening to me. I can tell. You've already made up your minds."

"That's not true, Eric . . ."

"Of course it's true. It's always true. It never matters what I think. Never! My opinion never counts for anything."

"That's not true, Eric."

"Then why don't you believe me about Owen? I wouldn't be his friend if he wasn't—I don't know. He's fantastic. He really is."

Mr. Nicholson cleared his throat and said, "Why do you need our permission now? Apparently you didn't need it before."

"The sculpture he was doing cracked. He has to start over. And, well, Owen asked me if I wanted to help him pick out the marble for the new one. See, it's kind of hard to explain, but . . ."

"Where would you go?" his father interjected.

"To a quarry, a special quarry—in Vermont. And he wants to make a trip out of it. And . . ."

The expression of shock on Mr. Nicholson's face made Eric stop talking. "Eric," he began softly, "I don't ever want you to see this—this *freak*—again. Do you understand me? Ever."

"He's not a freak!"

"I've never been so serious about anything in my life. If you do, I'll go up to that mountain and make him regret he ever laid eyes on you. Is that clear?"

"No! It's not clear. It's not . . ."

"Eric, I'm telling you—there's nothing more to discuss!"

"What do you mean? You can't just sit there and tell me I can't see Owen again! You can't! Because I'm going to see him—no matter what you say!"

"Now wait a minute, Lou—Eric," Mrs. Nicholson said. "This is getting out of hand. Eric, you have to try and understand what we're saying . . ."

"Oh, I understand. I understand perfectly. It's you two who don't!"

"Don't you see, Eric," Mrs. Nicholson went on. "This whole setup with you and Owen—well, it just doesn't make sense. Why would an old man who's lived alone for years suddenly want to go off on a trip to Vermont with a young boy?"

"Because we're friends! What's so difficult to understand about that?"

"I don't think it's just friendship, Eric," Mr. Nicholson said. "There are too many crazy, sick people in this world—and your friend up on that mountain, no matter what he seems to you, seems like a prime suspect for a crazy."

"But he's not, Dad! Talk to Chris's father. He knows Owen."

"I'm sorry, Eric. I'm going to have to insist on your promise that you won't go against me on this. I don't want you seeing him again."

"I have to go once more. I mean, I have to tell him . . ."

"Call him."

"He doesn't have a phone."

"Then write him a letter."

"Oh, God, Dad! You can't do this. You can't!"

"I know it seems hard now, Eric," Mrs. Nicholson said. "But if you just think about it . . ."

"No! I'm not going to think about it. And I'm not going to stop seeing Owen! Never . . ."

"Eric . . ."

"Shut up, Dad! Just shut up and leave me alone!" he screamed, running from the room.

"Get back here, Eric!" Mr. Nicholson ordered.

"Leave me alone!"

"Eric!"

He didn't answer. He pulled open the front door and ran outside.

"Where are you going?" his father demanded, running after him. "Get back here!"

Eric kept on running through the darkened streets. *Leave me alone. Just leave me alone!* he screamed to himself. He didn't realize where he was running until he found himself a few houses from Chris's. *I can't go there*, he panicked. *Dad'll go there right away. Oh, God, I can't go any place. Except Owen's . . . I can wait until they all go to bed, and then get my bike and ride out there . . .*

He could hear his father catching up to him and he hid behind a large tree, holding his breath until his father passed. *I hate you!* he screamed silently after him. *It's all your fault . . .*

The front light at Chris's house was suddenly switched on and Eric realized his father must have rung the Praeger's bell, thinking he'd gone there. *Boy, I bet you're embarrassed now. What are you going to say when they look at you like you're nuts?* He tried to laugh, but he couldn't. There was nothing to laugh about. Everything seemed so hopeless . . .

Finally he heard the Praeger's front door shutting, and then the sound of his father's footsteps. His father was walking now, slowly; and when he was almost to the tree, Eric stepped out.

"I'm here, Dad."

"Eric, is that you?"

"I'm here."

Mr. Nicholson reached toward him and grabbed Eric's shoulder. "Don't you ever run out like that again."

Eric pulled away. "I bet you didn't even talk to Mr. Praeger about Owen."

"What?"

"Well, you were there. You could have asked Chris's father about Owen. I told you he knew him."

"Owen was the farthest thing from my mind . . ."

"You could have at least asked him, Dad!"

Mr. Nicholson sighed angrily. Neither he nor Eric spoke until they were almost to the house. Suddenly Eric stopped walking and faced his father. "I just want you to know how much I hate you for this. I'll never forgive you."

"That's fine, Eric, so long as you don't ever see that man again. Is that clear?"

Eric felt his anger building, threatening to erupt at any minute, and he started quickly away across the front lawn.

Mr. Nicholson pulled him back. "I want this settled now. You've gotten your mother very upset."

"What about me? What do you think I am?"

"I want your promise, Eric."

"No."

Mr. Nicholson tightened his hold. "As far as I'm concerned, the matter is over and done with. Don't let me find you've been to that mountain—ever again." And letting go as roughly as he'd grabbed hold, he said, "Now get inside. I've really had it with you tonight."

Mrs. Nicholson was waiting for them at the door. "Eric, are you all right?"

"Oh, sure, Mom. I'm just terrific. I've never been better!"

Eric stood in front of the mailbox a long time the next morning, unable to decide whether to mail the letter to Owen. He must have rewritten it twenty-five times. It still wasn't right. But there was no best way to say what he had to say. And he dropped it in.

Dear Owen,

Everything is ruined. I can't go on the trip with you. And I can't come to see you anymore. My parents won't let me. I'm sorry. I really am. I wanted to go with you to the quarry more than anything. Maybe it's all my fault because I never really told them about you. But the reason I didn't is because I knew they would ruin everything just like they did. They've heard stories about your being a hermit and incredibly stupid things like that. I tried to explain, but I guess I didn't do a good job. It's so hard to explain. They wouldn't understand anyway. They don't understand anything! *I even told them to talk to Chris's father, but they said no. I really hate them for this, Owen. I hate them! I hate them! But right now I better not come out to see you. I wish I could so much. Maybe we'll run into each other in town. I* hope *so.*

Your friend,
Eric

"I should have gone out to see him. I should have told him myself. I still can. I can go right now," he mumbled as he turned from the mailbox. But he knew he wouldn't. And he knew it had nothing to do with his father. He knew he couldn't face Owen.

He'd planned on going to Chris's, but he'd only gone a few steps when he changed his mind. He couldn't face anyone now. Even Chris. Especially Chris. Chris would get him talking and he didn't want to talk. Or they'd go swimming or bike into town or someplace—maybe even Grosset Lake. And Chris would act incredibly stupid and funny until finally Eric would find himself laughing, feeling good, happy, alive again . . .

And he didn't want that.

"Owen!" Eric exclaimed as he answered the door after dinner the next night. He was surprised as much by the way Owen looked as by Owen's being there. His hair was neatly combed and his beard and mustache trimmed. He wore slacks, a shirt, jacket and tie.

"How do I look?" Owen whispered.

"Different."

"You don't like it?"

"I guess. I just have to get used to it."

"Don't try too hard. I hope I don't have to pull myself together like this again for a long time. At least, I don't think your father will toss me out right away!"

"Didn't you get my letter?" Eric asked seriously.

"That's why I'm here. I have to speak with your parents."

"I don't know, Owen . . ."

"Aren't they home?"

"Yes. But I don't think they want to see you."

"I don't expect they do."

"Dad was pretty mad."

"So was I. Now go ahead and tell them I'm here."

"Okay." Eric shrugged. Then he said, "Are you sure, Owen? You don't know my father."

"Do you want me to leave?"

Eric thought for a moment, and said, "I don't know."

"Are you scared?"

Eric sighed. "I think so."

Owen smiled and looked long at Eric. "Yes, I think I am, too. But some of the best things in life you have to struggle for, my friend. It's up to you. I'll go if you want."

Eric thought for a moment, then called, "Mom! Dad! Somebody's here to see you."

"Who is it?" Mrs. Nicholson called back.

Eric hesitated a moment, and Owen answered for him. "It's Owen Cassell."

Eric's mother reached the bottom of the stairs at the same moment his father appeared from the kitchen. They both stood speechless, staring. Eric was terrified. He thought his father might just punch Owen.

"I think we have to talk, Mr. Nicholson," Owen said in a friendly, easy way.

"Who are you?" came a small voice from the staircase. It was Buddy. Kathy was standing behind him, gaping at Owen.

"You must be Buddy. My name is Owen."

"You mean Stoneface," Kathy giggled under her breath.

"Who's Stoneface?" Buddy exclaimed.

"Eric, I want you and Kathy to take Buddy upstairs," Mrs. Nicholson said quickly. "It's his bedtime."

"If you don't mind, I'd like Eric to be in on this, too." Owen said.

Eric held his breath while his parents exchanged a look. "Kathy, you put Buddy to bed, then," Mr. Nicholson said.

"Oh, Daddy, can't I stay, too?"

"Kathy," her father warned. "And stay upstairs when you're finished."

"But I wanted to watch TV."

"Not tonight," he said brusquely.

"Oh, boy," Kathy moaned. "Come on," she snapped to Buddy.

Buddy started to whimper.

"Go on now. I'll be up to tuck you in," Mrs. Nicholson promised. Turning to Owen, she said, "We can talk in the living room."

Owen sat on the couch. Mr. and Mrs. Nicholson sat in chairs opposite him. Eric stood behind his mother's chair.

"Well." Mr. Nicholson cleared his throat. "I'd say this was a little late in coming."

"I just received Eric's letter this morning. It upset me very much. I spent the day trying to sort it all out."

"You're not the only one," Mr. Nicholson shot back.

"I think you are operating under some very powerful misconceptions."

"That was Eric's supposition, too."

"Mr. Nicholson, I'm a very private person. I've lived

alone for the past twenty-four years. It isn't easy for me coming here tonight, but I couldn't figure out an alternative. At the very least, you owe me the courtesy of hearing me out."

"That's your opinion. I think I've extended myself just letting you in my house!"

"I understand your fears about my relationship with Eric, Mr. Nicholson. If my son had come to me with the story I imagine Eric told you, I probably would have reacted in much the same way. I am as aware as the next person of how people in this town view me. I'm sure that . . ."

"My wife and I couldn't care less about local gossip, Cassell. We simply didn't like what Eric told us—or didn't tell us."

"Would you have reacted so strongly if Eric had struck up a friendship with an elderly neighbor of yours who spent his days rocking on the front porch and tending to his vegetable garden? The fact that I'm that crazy Owen Cassell, Stoneface, the old hermit who lives with his stone people on a mountain miles out of town—that makes the difference."

Mr. Nicholson thought for a moment, then nodded. "I guess that about puts it in a nutshell, Cassell."

"I'd like to tell you something of myself and why I've chosen to live the way I have . . ."

"I'm not really interested."

"Dad!" Eric burst out, but his father's angry look immediately silenced him.

"But you are interested in using a distorted version to turn Eric against me," Owen went on.

"I don't see the point in this—"

"Lou, let him speak," Mrs. Nicholson said. And looking at Owen, she continued, "Go ahead, Mr. Cassell. I'd like to hear."

Owen sighed deeply, stole a glance at Eric, and began: "Twenty-four years ago I lost my family. My wife and son died in a fire that destroyed my home. I tell you this not to play on your sympathies, but because it is the reason why I am what I am today. It is impossible to explain the profound changes such a loss creates in a person's life. Perhaps there are people who can pick up the pieces and start all over again. I couldn't. Besides my work, my wife and son were my life. And it was, I believe, a life as complete as a person can hope for.

"But the night of the fire, my son, Michael, and I had had an argument—a real blowup over his buying a car. He'd just turned sixteen, and was saving up his own money. I thought he was too young for a car, and my wife felt he wasn't. The three of us argued terribly all through dinner. Sometimes I think that hurts more than anything else—Michael and I got along so well, better than most fathers and sons probably; and yet, the night he died we were so angry with each other—over buying a car. It seems ridiculous now . . ."

Owen paused for a moment, seeming far away; and Mrs. Nicholson reached up to take hold of Eric's hand, squeezing it reassuringly.

"I went out after dinner to walk and clear my mind, to think over the whole fool problem of the car. I walked for hours. I often do. It was a clear, magnificent late March night. The moon was so bright and the stars so thick they almost blotted out the darkness. I suppose I thought about a lot of other things besides Michael and the car. Who knows? It doesn't matter. It's so easy to get caught up on the mountain in a night like that, to lose oneself. On such nights I forget about time, sleep—all the things which bind us to the earth—and wander till dawn sometimes. Perhaps I would have that night if I hadn't seen the flames . . . But by the time I got there, it was too late . . .

"And afterwards, there was nothing. No one to live with, no one to love, no one to laugh and cry with—nothing, except my work, my sculptures. At first, though, even they were unbearable. I sold off some of what I had and discarded the rest. I couldn't stand having them around, constant reminders of what my life was before.

"I thought I would never work again. It seemed impossible without Celia—my wife—until I realized I could in some way bring her back through the stone. The stone has life, you see . . ." He paused, as though groping for words. "Not life as we imagine life to be. Rather something very basic to creation, to the earth. Most people think that rock is dead—but it isn't. And I think . . . no, I know—" and he looked at Eric and smiled—"I know Eric feels that, too . . . As a sculptor, I feel I'm in constant struggle with the earth. It's as though she wants to keep this life for herself. She dares us to touch it, to mold it and give form to its beauty. Whether the artist succeeds in this struggle or not doesn't negate the life. It's there. It's always there.

"When at last I began working on my sculpture of Celia, I knew the stone was working with me. Everything flowed, as if she were still there, helping me along, as if she were longing to have the sculpture finished, to be with me again. But it was different with Michael. His life, his essence, constantly evaded me. Finally I couldn't even remember what he looked like. I'd sit and stare at the stone. I knew it was there, I knew the life within the stone was Michael if I could only capture it. But I couldn't. I had nothing to work with, no image—until I saw Eric.

"If I had a picture of Michael, you would be startled at the resemblance. I tell you, when I saw Eric the first time, I felt as though I had entered a time lapse—it was my son walking down the street. Of course, that lasted only a few moments, but seeing Eric made my mind begin to work again. I craved the stone. After twenty years I knew I had a chance of finishing the sculpture of Michael.

"At first I watched Eric from afar. I didn't know how to approach him. I thought I might frighten him, and I had to watch him as he really is, not some self-conscious version. But I suppose I'm not a good spy—Eric caught on to me. Yet instead of being frightened or laughing at me as crazy old Stoneface, he chose to be my friend. Believe me, it shocked me as much as it must have shocked you. I never thought I would have a friend again, and certainly not a fourteen-year-old boy. I thought I would live out my life content with my stone people, as Eric calls them." He smiled. "Sometimes I think it is the stone people who are Eric's true friends. I believe the flaw in the Michael sculpture caused him more pain than it did even me. That's why I want to bring him with me to the quarry. I want him to see it. It's where it all begins, the source . . ."

He stopped abruptly, as though suddenly aware of where he was, and shook his head sadly. "I suppose you think I'm mad, don't you? I came here with all sorts of arguments to convince you that I was of fit moral fiber to be a companion to Eric, and all I've done is rave on . . ."

"No, no! Not at all!" Mrs. Nicholson insisted. "I just can't believe Eric is caught up in it as much as you say . . ."

"What does that mean?" Eric demanded.

"Your interests usually run from baseball to soccer to football to basketball to hockey—depending on the season," she reminded him.

Eric frowned. "What's wrong with that?"

"Nothing. Nothing at all."

There was a long silence and finally Mr. Nicholson spoke. "I still don't understand. You talk about all this being important to Eric, but it seems to me it's just as important to you. Maybe more."

Owen seemed surprised. "I've never denied that. I couldn't."

"Have you ever asked yourself why?"

Owen nodded thoughtfully. "Yes, many times. I am seventy-one years old. Eric is fourteen. And yet there is an undeniable bond between us, a friendship as deep and true as any I've known . . ." He sat forward and rested his arms on his knees. Looking at Eric, he went on. "At first I thought Eric had become a substitute for Michael. And although I'm sure that's a part of it—I'd be a fool to deny it—I know the answer is not so simple. Love is never simple . . ." He paused. "And I don't use the word lightly. I care about Eric. I receive immense joy from sharing emotions and experiences with him. I'm delighted when something I say makes him smile with wonder and starts his mind working. I love the questions he asks me and the places our conversations take us. It sometimes brings tears to my eyes when I think that my sculpture and all I value in my life and in my work have affected Eric as deeply as they have . . ."

Owen paused again. Eric looked from him to his mother, who smiled softly, to his father, whose head was bent over as he stared at his hands.

"It's a sad fact of life," Owen went on, "that we are conditioned to fear love when it comes to us in unexpected times and forms. But just because I am old and have lived my life in a way which is different from yours, and because Eric is young, I don't see why the emotional bond between us is something to fear. I sometimes think it is the memory of the love I had with my wife and son which has kept me alive all these years. I know how precious it is and I cherish it all the more in Eric. Joy, caring, and sharing in another human being is something which doesn't happen often in life. Perhaps that's why Eric was afraid to tell you about our friendship. I think the strength of the emotions he feels is something new, something he's not quite sure what to do with. His letter made me realize how much I needed to talk with you—for his sake and mine, too. I didn't know I had some of these thoughts until today."

Owen glanced toward Mr. Nicholson, and when their eyes met, he went on: "I don't mean to sit here and tell you how to bring up your son, but it seems to me that if we can't discuss this without anger and hostility, then the message we are ultimately giving Eric is: beware of your feelings, don't trust them, keep them locked up inside . . ." Owen sighed deeply, and closing his eyes a moment, he added, "And I know, believe me I know, how painful that is . . ."

The room was very still after Owen stopped talking. It was a gentle, calming stillness; and as Eric glanced from his father to his mother, he could feel himself relaxing. He knew Owen had accomplished the impossible: before the evening was over, his parents would agree to the quarry trip.

Ξ

Eric stood with Owen at the edge of the quarry, staring in disbelief at its jagged cliffs of white-gray rock that plunged down hundreds of feet into a pool of still, green water. It was a creepy place. The quarry was deserted, and it frightened him.

"What's happened?" he breathed.

Owen didn't answer. He seemed not to have heard as he stared into the distance.

Eric looked again, hoping to find something to make him feel better, something of what they'd come to see. The quarry was nothing as he had imagined: no polished, shining bowl of white, stone people marble, no magical birthplace for the stone boy. Owen had told him stories of men who had worked the quarry—Big Red Jenkins, Al Copeland, Sy Lawson, Jonah Weyland and others—men who had grown in Eric's imagination into giants wielding massive iron hammers on long iron rods, splitting the marble, pounding the earth with a deafening beat. But there were no men working here. They were gone, vanished, leaving this enormous, deathlike silence . . .

"I can almost hear it still," Owen said suddenly, startling Eric, as if reading his thoughts.

"Hear what?"

Owen smiled as he continued to gaze across the quarry.

Eric followed his gaze this time, hoping to see what Owen saw, but there were only large, flat, ugly quarry buildings sparkling in the summer sun.

"Hear what?" Eric asked again.

"The sound of the men struggling to take the stone, groaning, sweating, pounding the earth. The sound of the iron hammers against the stone, and of the earth finally giving up. It echoes still . . ."

Eric listened. He wanted to hear what Owen heard; but there was nothing, only the unnatural silence of the place. It seemed to swell up from below the green water, filling the quarry and spilling over the edge.

"You used to be able to hear it being worked for miles," Owen went on. "Some was done by machine; but Wally loved the stone, so most of the cutting was done by hand. That's why I came here. It was hard to find a quarry that hand cut even then. There's a difference . . ."

Eric found himself looking down into the pool of still water, as if the answers, the memories—whatever it was Owen knew and heard—could be found there. But the pool was so far down, so dark, so silent, it seemed unreal or trapped, threatening to swallow Eric into its murky depths, and he stepped back suddenly.

"You know what I think, Owen?"

"What?"

"I think that if somebody came and murdered us right now and threw our bodies in there, nobody would ever find us."

Owen laughed. "No, I don't suppose they would. But I can think of worse places to spend eternity."

"Wow, you are weird, Owen! I mean, sometimes you're weirder than other times."

"Thank you!"

"Oh, no! This place is making us both looney. Come on." He pulled at Owen's arm. "Let's get out of here!"

"No, now I'm serious. I think I like the quarry even better now that it's abandoned. No, abandon's not the right word. It's been abandoned only by people. For years the stone was cut into day in and day out—cut into and taken away, but never destroyed. Look how the grass and bush are growing in the crevices of the rock. Wild flowers cling up and down the quarry walls. Even the water seems to have its place, as though nature is slowly reclaiming her own—what people have found cause to abandon and forget. It's as it should be. Come on, let's climb down."

"I don't know . . ."

"It's wonderful down below—a vast and awesome world looking up from the bottom. All you see is stone and sky." Owen smiled. "An enormous egg of stone and sky . . ."

"An egg?"

Owen nodded. "Michael once described it that way when he was very small."

"Okay, but you go first!"

They were halfway down the quarry cliff when a loud, angry voice demanded, "What do you think you're doing? This is private property! Can't you read the signs?"

Eric and Owen looked up. An old man was standing at the top of the quarry, a dog growling by his side. The sun sparkled brightly off the barrel of the old man's gun.

"Wally!" Owen cried out, waving madly. "Wally? Is that you? It's me, Owen! Owen Cassell!"

"You say Owen Cassell? Is that what I heard?" the old man shouted.

"You heard right, Wally." And turning to Eric, Owen said, "Come on. It's Wally."

"Well, I'll be—Owen!" Wally cried, extending his hand as Owen reached the edge of the quarry. "I thought you was dead!"

"Wally, my God, it's good to see you! I must admit I thought the same!"

Wally laughed. "Not me! Not by a long shot! This old body ain't what it used to be, but I'm fit enough to keep you or anyone else out of my quarry."

"I bet you are, old friend. I just bet you are!"

"Me and Bill." Wally grinned, tapping the dog. "Bill, I want you to meet Owen and . . ." He stopped abruptly, staring at Eric. Then he looked bewilderedly at Owen.

"Yes, I know. He looks a lot like Michael. This is Eric Nicholson. He and I are friends."

"Not related?"

"No!" Eric laughed.

"Well, I'll be!"

"But I've told him all about the quarry, Wally."

"Yeah?" Wally smiled proudly. "But then I guess you would, Owen." And turning to Eric the old man went on, "Told you about old Wally, eh? And how I taught him to cut the marble? Oh, but we had times together, didn't we, Owen? That's all I have left now—times past, when all was different. I hold on to it like an old fool. Come out here sometimes and walk the edge, me and Bill, imagining it all the way she used to be when old man Kempt was around. I see the men and hear them working. And I think, 'You're crazy, Wally. Your mind's just slipping. And someday you're gonna slip all the way and you ain't never gonna come out of the past.' " He smiled. "And I think that wouldn't be so bad, you know?"

"I know, I know all too well, my friend. Sometimes the

past . . ." But Owen stopped himself, and glancing quickly at Eric, he said, "No, I used to think all I had was in the past, but no longer. I need a piece of marble, Wally. Something special, of course."

"Of course!"

"Are there any places where . . ."

"What's the matter with here?"

"And how are two old men like you and me going to get marble out of your quarry?"

"Don't need to. I got some stored away. I had some of the best pieces hauled up just before we closed. Other people like you have come back over the years. Sculptors, I mean. You're the ones who know. But I got a piece, the best, saved for you. The minute I saw it, I put your name on it. Owen Cassell, I say. Only in my mind, of course. I knowed you'd be back some day. I was just hoping it'd be before I was gone."

As they walked through the dry grass at the quarry's rim, Wally stopped often to catch his breath or point out something of interest to Eric. When Wally stopped, Bill stopped, too, and sat at his feet, looking up at the old man.

"Did Owen ever tell you about the time we had a softball game at the bottom—right down there?" Wally pointed to the water.

"No kidding," Eric said, shaking his head.

Owen and Wally laughed as they remembered.

And Wally began, "Yep, it was on my fiftieth birthday. And Big Red—you remember him, don't you, Owen? . . ."

"Fine dinner with good friends. I'll sleep well tonight," Wally said as he got up to leave the campfire.

"Thanks to you. Those fish were your catch," Owen reminded him.

"Yeah, we would have starved on what Owen and I caught!" Eric laughed.

"Just blind luck though," Owen insisted.

"So you say!" Wally chuckled. "I was always the better fisherman!"

"Eric—my friend lies. I can remember times when we would fish all day over in Blue Pond, and Michael and I would . . ."

"Once! That happened only once, and I was sick. Coming down with a stomach virus, I was."

Owen laughed. "All right, Wally. Have it your way."

"It's not my way—it's the truth! And tomorrow morning breakfast's on me."

"No, no. I promised Eric bacon and eggs over an open fire."

"Good enough. I'll be back as soon as I smell the coffee. Goodnight now. And sleep well. I almost envy you sleeping out on a night like this."

"You can stay with us, Wally."

"Thanks, Eric, but that looks like a two-man tent. And besides, I don't think these old bones would take too kindly to the ground. I'll see you in the morning. Come on, Bill."

"I like Wally," Eric said as he watched the old man and his dog disappear into the darkness beyond the glow of the fire.

"Yes, and he likes you. But I'm not surprised."

"You know what surprised me?"

"No."

"The fish. I didn't want to tell you, but usually I don't like fish. Tonight it was really good."

"That's because it's so fresh. And you caught it and cleaned it yourself."

"I could do without the cleaning!"

"Next time I'll bring my butler!"

"Okay!" Eric laughed, looking up at the sky. "It's amazing."

"What?"

"All those stars. I've never seen so many."

"It only seems that way because the sky is so open here and the ground so flat."

"The quarry's a fantastic place, Owen."

"Then you don't feel like you're going to be murdered anymore?"

"No! That was stupid. Maybe I felt like that because it's so different here from what I'd imagined."

"And what did you imagine?'

"You'll laugh."

"Never."

"Well, I thought it was going to be something like—well, something like a big, shining bowl of stone people marble, all white and smooth."

Owen answered him, but to Eric he seemed suddenly far away, drifting beyond the flickering shadows of the fire. *Or maybe it's me,* Eric thought happily. And he leaned back on the ground, closing his eyes. He felt drowsy from all the food, the heat of the fire, and the day. What a day it had been—*And it could have been so terrible. It would have been with anyone but Owen. I can just imagine Mom and Dad if we'd traveled all this way to see a place and it was closed down—closed down . . .* He smiled. *Closed down to the whole world but Owen and me and Wally . . . It's nice the way Owen and Wally are still friends after all these years. You can tell they really like each other. I wonder if Chris and I will still be friends when we're seventy. Seventy!*

It was hard to imagine Chris and him ever being that old. He thought of the night before and how Chris had lent him his sleeping bag, and how, when they tried to roll it tight on the floor of Eric's room, they'd ended up laughing uncontrollably because of something Chris said: "And don't get *stoned* up there at that quarry. The first time's with me!" It was a terrible joke, but it seemed so funny at the time.

Eric looked toward Owen, thinking of telling him the joke anyway, but Owen was still talking about the quarry. Eric tried to listen, but Owen's words seemed to float above the glow of the fire into the stillness of the night, then vanish as if sucked up by the silence of the quarry—silence growing more and more intense, seeming to swell up from below the still, green pool, flooding Eric's mind as it blocked out the noises of the night: the crickets, the owls, the crackling of the fire and Owen's voice. *Owen probably wouldn't think the joke was funny anyway. He probably wouldn't even understand,* Eric decided, closing his eyes again, letting himself drift with the sensations of the night quarry.

I'd like to come here with Chris someday. Just Chris and me. Wally'll let us camp here. We'll catch fish and clean them, cook them like we did tonight . . . go swimming and dive off the quarry cliffs. If Chris thought the cliffs at Grosset Lake were big—wait till he sees these. Maybe if Chris were here, I could have dived from even higher today—Chris and me . . . Maybe we could dive from the quarry edge! His stomach tightened even at the thought of diving from that high up. But he'd been queasy the first time he dived from the cliffs at Grosset Lake.

It'd be something to dive in from the quarry edge—an Olympic dive! he thought happily, imagining himself standing next to Chris, the sun shining, sparkling off the quarry walls, so hot he could almost feel it—hotter than today. The kind of hot that makes you think if you don't dive in the water, you'll just burn up—

—"Ready!" He hears Chris calling, sees Chris grinning, daring him to dive in.

"We could get killed you know."

"No! Not us! We're going to take off like birds and fly right down to the water!"

"You sure?"

"I'm sure!" Chris is standing in the sunlight at the quarry edge, smiling, daring him . . .

"Okay. You're on!"

"Now!"

The takeoff is perfect. Eric feels it. They're together all the way, floating out over the quarry, clear of the gray-white cliffs, up into the air a moment and then down, a sweet, smooth ride down, carried along by the warm breeze, coasting down, down past the white-gray cliffs, past the wild flowers, gliding into the still, green water, so cool, so silky against his skin. Down, down they swim, effortlessly, to the depths of the quarry where the walls are polished to a satiny white finish and the water sparkles like sunlight reflecting off shimmering marble.

"The cave. It's like the cave." Eric smiles because he's talking under water. And then he realizes Chris knows nothing about the cave. "But you will," he promises. "I have to show you Owen's cave."

Chris does a dolphin-like backwards somersault and motions Eric down further. They swim side by side, almost touching, until they reach the quarry floor; swerving suddenly upwards, soaring with incredible speed, bursting from the still green depths into the bright warmth of day, upwards toward the blue sky . . .

The sense of daring, the exhilaration of the dive lingered with Eric, making his senses feel alive. Chris seemed with him, as if he were sitting nearby with Owen, talking, laughing, smiling through the soft glow of the fire; but when Eric opened his eyes, he was alone. Owen was standing at the quarry edge. After a while, Eric got up and stood silently beside him.

"I first came here forty-nine years ago," Owen said. "A lifetime. It seems impossible. And yet, it's all here. My life is as much a part of this place as are the lives of the stone people. Sometimes I think it's where it all began . . ."

Owen's words echoed in Eric's ears, and he peered into the black depths of the quarry, thinking, *It's where it all began. The stone people were once a part of all this. They could have come from any place. From fifty feet in the air below us. From where we walked this afternoon. From a wall I touched . . . From below the water—from where the quarry sparkles . . .* He smiled to himself.

"What a night it is." Owen spoke softly. "I wouldn't trade it for any other. It's like the cave opened up to the sky. Boundless and still, yet not beyond reach . . . The quarry is very much alive tonight."

Eric knew Owen was right. The quarry *was* alive tonight, a living place where the sound of men working, the smell of their sweat and the distant moan of the earth rose up from below the still, green pool, rising in a soft, low moan, so faint and far away it might not have existed at all except in Eric's mind. Slowly, so slowly, the moan grew until the earth trembled with the work of thousands of unseen men cutting into the marble. Tap, tap, pause . . . Tap, tap, pause—thousands of unseen men, thousands of unseen hammers, thousands of unseen chisels working together as one, polishing the quarry walls until they sparkled as sunlight reflected off shimmering marble, echoing like a symphony from the center of the earth.

"Do you hear it, Owen? Do you hear it?" he whispered.

"Hear what?"

"It's the quarry. I can hear the men working. I can."

"What does it sound like?"

"It's all these instruments playing, but it's not instruments. It's so crazy, Owen. It's the men working. And it's coming from the quarry. You hear it, don't you?"

"I can't hear it," Owen whispered, putting his arm around Eric's shoulder. "It's only for you. This is your time, my friend . . ."

Eric was diving again, flying through the air, feeling free, incredibly free. "I wish Chris were here right now . . ." he blurted out.

"To hear the stone music?"

Eric was embarrassed. He didn't know what he meant, and he said, "Do you think he could?"

"It's what you think that matters."

Eric didn't know what he thought. Instead, he found himself asking, "Owen, do you remember what you said about the cave? About having to experience it to understand it?"

"Yes."

"I want to show Chris the cave."

Owen hesitated before answering, "If you like. But I'd prefer if you didn't spread the word to all your friends—a place like the cave can be so easily destroyed."

"Oh, I know. I wouldn't tell anyone else!"

"Of course, then. Bring Chris any time . . ."

Ξ

"But you didn't dive from the top of the quarry?" Chris asked.

"Are you kidding? It's much higher than Grosset Lake."

"How far did you dive from?"

"I don't know. It's hard to tell . . ."

"Higher than Grosset Lake?" Chris persisted.

"Maybe . . ."

"Sure!"

"There was no moral support, you know—only Owen and Wally telling me to be careful, and . . ."

"A likely story!" Chris grinned.

Eric leaned back in his chair, shaking his head. Maybe he had dived from higher than he and Chris had at Grosset Lake, but there was no way he could convince Chris. And absent-mindedly he picked up a piece of marble Wally had given him. It was perfectly round and polished to a smooth white finish like the stone people. "You have to understand the quarry, Chris. It's nothing like a lake—no feeling of wide-open space. It's a big hole dug into the ground and it's filled with water now. But somehow, the water doesn't look like it belongs there. And there's something about the quiet—it's like the water. You can't help noticing it. And you feel very far away from the rest of the world. Like it might feel on Mars or someplace in space . . ."

"Sounds like you got stoned anyway!"

Eric turned the marble over and over in his hand. "If being stoned is anything like being at the quarry, then I'm all for it!"

"What's that?" Chris pointed to the marble.

"Just a piece of marble Wally gave me," Eric said, handing it to Chris.

"Is this what the quarry looks like?"

"No, it's mostly gray rock. Wally polished it."

Chris nodded. "It's nice . . ."

"You want it?" Eric said. But as soon as he'd spoken, he felt embarrassed. What would Chris want with a piece of stone?

Chris smiled. "Yeah. Thanks," he said.

And Eric found himself telling Chris about the stone music. He hadn't planned to. It just seemed right. "I know it sounds weird—music from a stone quarry!" Eric exclaimed as he finished. "But it sounded so real. I swear it did . . ."

"Wow, that's incredible! Really incredible!"

"You should have been there and heard it! You know, we really have to go there together someday . . ."

"I don't mean the music. I mean, well—you heard it on the first night you were away? Right?"

Eric nodded.

Chris rolled his eyes. "You're not going to believe this, but—I went to the mountain *that* night!"

"Stoneface?"

"Where else?"

"What for?"

"I don't know, Eric! I really don't. That's what's so weird! I'd told Bauer I might stop over after supper, but when I got to his house, he wasn't there. And with both you and Arnold away—I don't know, maybe I was bored or something—but all of a sudden I found myself thinking about the stone boy. I'd never seen him, and Bauer's house is already halfway to the reservoir."

"But what did you want to see him for with his face half gone?"

"I didn't think about that. I just kept on thinking . . ." He shrugged and grinned. "I don't know what I was thinking! But I rode like crazy all the way out there. If I was thinking anything, it was, 'What am I doing? Owen's not even there!'—you know, stuff like that. But I kept on going. And then when I got up there, everything was so quiet. Kind of spooky—there I was on Stoneface all alone. I'd never been there alone. And—wow, does this sound weird or what?"

"No weirder than the stone music!"

"Yeah, I guess. But you know what was the strangest? When I saw the statue . . . I kept on feeling that you were going to start—I mean, that the statue—was going to start talking to me any minute. So I stayed there in the garden for I don't know how long, thinking all these weird things."

"You're finally hooked!"

"I think that's what I was thinking—'Here I am as crazy as Eric and Owen!' "

They both laughed.

"I told you you should have come to the mountain sooner," Eric said. "Wait till Owen hears . . ."

"Hey, no—don't tell Owen."

"Why?"

"Maybe he wouldn't like the idea of me going out to his place when he wasn't there."

"Because of Halloween?"

"I guess . . ."

"He's forgotten all about that."

"I don't know . . ." Chris shrugged.

"Come on. Hey, there's this cave behind the face in the mountain. Owen took me there. It's the most incredible place I've ever seen, besides maybe the quarry. It was sacred to the Indians. They said the spirit of Stoneface lives there. Owen believes it. And I think maybe I do too."

"You're kidding."

"I can't explain it. It's something you have to experience. You want to go sometime?"

"Do I get to meet this spirit personally?"

"The way you're going—you just might!"

"When do you want to go?"

"Tomorrow?"

"Why not?"

"Okay by me . . ."

They didn't go to the cave then. The marble was delivered, and it took the two delivery men, Owen, Eric and Chris almost two hours to maneuver the huge stone across the burned-out rubble and position it to Owen's satisfaction in the garden. By that time, they were too tired, hot and hungry to think of climbing the mountain. Instead they had lunch with Owen in the cabin.

"How's your father, Chris?" Owen asked as they sat down to eat. "I haven't seen him lately."

"Oh, he's okay. I guess he's been kind of busy."

"Does he ever talk to you about Michael, my son?"

"Not much. But . . ."

"They were very close, you know."

"I know that. He said Michael was the best friend he ever had. He's got this picture of him and Michael on his dresser—you know, where he keeps a lot of pictures of me and my brother and my mother. But he's got the one of Michael there, too. They have these baseball hats on and they're both making dopey faces."

"Oh, yes!" Owen exclaimed. "I remember the picture. I believe I took it. It was on the day their Little League team won the league championship. They must have been eleven or twelve. I didn't know your father had that picture."

"Sure. I could bring it to you sometime. I'm sure Dad wouldn't mind."

"Yes, I'd like that very much. Your father spent a lot of time here. He and Michael were friends for a long time. In fact, they were planning on buying a car together, and traveling across country when they graduated."

"Is that the car you and Michael had the fight over?" Eric asked. He knew Owen wouldn't mind.

Owen nodded. "They had it all picked out—a 1947 Plymouth. Belonged to an old man named Fenway, who lived over on Crestview Drive. He wanted $175 for it. Doesn't sound like much now, but it was a lot of money in those days, especially for two young boys. But it wasn't a bad price for the car. Old Fenway had kept it spotless . . ." Owen sighed. "Funny the kind of details you remember . . ."

"How come you didn't want them to buy it?" Eric asked.

"Oh, well, I suppose I was just being a parent—as your parents were when they first said no to the trip."

"What happened? Dad's never told me about this," Chris said.

"Well, your father's parents had agreed to the car. My wife thought it was a fine idea, too. I was the only one who didn't. Perhaps I would have changed my mind, but I didn't have the chance. Michael died first. I remember it so clearly, Chris, because we argued over the car the night of the fire."

"I'm sorry . . ."

"Sorry?" Owen shook his head, smiling sadly. "No need to be sorry . . . It's strange, though—your father and I never talk about Michael. He's in our thoughts whenever we see each other. And we always seem to talk around him. I'm sorry about that . . . I suppose that's my fault. Your father never talked to you about the fire?"

"He's told me some. He said the only things left really were the statues."

Owen nodded, and reached for his sketch pad and pen before going on. "I remember your father came up here shortly after the fire. I don't think he expected to see me. I was staying in town at the time. He got here first. When I arrived, he was sitting next to the statue of Michael, the one of Michael in the garden now, of him as a child. Anyway, your father's back was to me, and I couldn't tell who it was. So many people came out here after the fire—just to look. People who had no right here. I thought your father was one of them. And I started yelling, ready to throw him bodily off the mountain. And then your father turned around and started to apologize. My mind was so confused. I didn't know what he was apologizing for. It seemed he was apologizing for Michael's death. And I began yelling again. I don't even know what I was saying. Your father looked frightened. I suppose I appeared as a mad man. It was one of those strange moments in life—there were so many memories of Michael in your father, Chris. I think I wanted nothing more than to put my arms around him and cry. He would have understood. Perhaps at that moment, he was the only one who would have understood—'I'm sorry, Owen. I'm sorry,' he kept on saying. He was just a boy himself. And I don't know, perhaps it was that I couldn't stand seeing him alive—but I made it impossible for him. Finally he left. I didn't see him for months. Yet the memory of that day stayed with me. I realized he probably needed me as much as I needed him. And I went to his house, to apologize. But by that time it was too late. We've never spoken of Michael since."

Owen drew while he talked, his hand moving deftly over the paper. "But let's talk about more cheerful things. We must celebrate the arrival of the new stone."

Again and again the conversation returned to Michael and sometimes to Michael and Chris's father. Owen told stories Eric had never heard about Owen's life before the fire, nothing mysterious or magical such as stories of life within the stone, or Indian caves or quarries where the earth speaks—ordinary family memories, the kind Eric could imagine his parents telling. And Owen sketched all the time they talked. Sometimes he spent only a minute on a page before flipping it over. Other times he'd labor over a page, finally tearing it from the pad, crumbling it and throwing it on the floor.

"Can we see what you've been drawing?" Chris asked when it was time to leave.

"Certainly," Owen said, handing the pad to Chris.

Eric moved his chair closer. He was used to seeing Owen's sketches, but Chris examined each page slowly; he sounded amazed at the details Owen had chosen to sketch over and over. Two pages were filled with hands, Eric's hands, held in different positions.

"These are really neat," Chris said. "I've never seen drawings like them. It's like you're looking at each part of Eric, sort of like a skeleton."

"Yes, that's true. First the skeleton, then the muscles and finally the flesh. I have to know it all."

Chris kept turning the pages, but stopped when he came to a sketch of himself.

"Hey, that's you!" Eric exclaimed.

"So it is!" Chris grinned, and he turned another page.

"Well, what do you know? It's you and me!" Eric said.

"I never realized how much you resemble your father, Chris," Owen said. "Perhaps it's seeing you with Eric. I've had the strangest sensation on and off all afternoon of being back in time, talking with Michael and your father. Twenty-four years seemed to vanish."

"I wonder what Dad would think. Hey, Owen, could I borrow this?"

"Of course. But there are more. Pick any you like."

Laughing, Eric suggested, "Hey, don't tell your father it's you and me right away. See what he says first!"

"Yeah. Maybe this will change his mind."

"About what?" Owen asked.

"Talking to you about Michael. And then I could tell him you want to."

Owen smiled sadly. "Thank you, Chris. I'd prefer you didn't. Maybe when your father comes again. Maybe that will be the right time."

Owen began work on the new marble the next morning. As the weeks went by he became so involved in the stone, he sometimes barely noticed when Eric arrived or left. Eric found himself staying away from the mountain more and more—Owen didn't seem to mind—and there was so much to do with Chris: summer was almost over, school was starting soon, and time no longer seemed endless . . .

Afternoon on the Mountain

The wind had heaped the snow near the cabin, piling it in drifts so high, it reached halfway up the windows. Eric stood at the door a moment, before hesitantly raising his hand to knock. He'd never knocked before. He'd always barged right in. Still, it had been so many years. And his hand fell against the door.

There was no answer.

He knocked again, harder.

Still no answer.

Maybe he's sleeping. He reached for the latch and as the door swung wide, Eric called, "Owen! It's me, Eric! I'm back!"

The cabin was dark and empty. The bed was made, the dishes done and the worktable piled neatly with sketches. The stove was cold. Eric shivered, feeling confused and disoriented, as if he'd opened a wrong door and found himself on the edge of a world he did not know.

Turning suddenly, he called out across the wind-swept meadow, "Owen? Where are you? It's me, Eric. I'm back!" He called again and again, until his throat hurt and he was shivering uncontrollably. *I'll start a fire. Owen will see the smoke from the chimney and come back. Then everything will be the same . . .* he assured himself as he fumbled with the wood and carried it inside.

It wasn't until the fire caught that he relaxed, settling back in his old chair, close to the open stove. His body began to tingle with a new warmth, and he kicked off his boots to warm his feet on the stone underneath the stove. It seemed so long since he'd left his bike against the snow-covered jeep at the end of Old Reservoir Road. *Years ago . . .* He smiled, gazing about the room softened now by the lamplight and filled with the scent of the burning wood. The old magic was still very much alive here, a sense of Owen and the boy Eric had been five years before.

Coffee—that's what I need, he thought, noticing the coffeepot in its old place by the sink. The coffee too, was right where Eric remembered; and while he waited for it to brew, he sat at the worktable, looking through the sketches. There were many he had never seen before, faces of strangers, although there were many new ones of Celia and some of himself.

When the coffee was ready, Eric poured himself a cup and returned to the worktable. His eye caught some sketches tacked to the wall. Among them were several Owen had drawn of Eric and Chris that day before school started, when they'd spent the afternoon with Owen. Eric took one down and gazed at it for a long time . . .

That Autumn

"GUESS WHAT I FOUND UNDER A WHOLE BUNCH OF JUNK on my desk?" Chris asked as he and Eric walked to school.

"What?"

"This!" Chris pulled the sketch Owen had made of them from his notebook.

"Hey, I forgot all about that! Did you ever show it to your father?"

"Not until last night. I forgot about it, too."

"What did he say?"

"At first he just sat and stared at it. Then he asked, in this funny voice, 'Where'd you find this?' "

"What did you tell him?"

"All about Owen and you. And I told him some of what Owen told us that day the marble was delivered. I hope it's okay."

"What did he say?"

"He really opened up. He talked to me like he'd never talked before. He told me all these things about him and Owen's son, and that trip they were planning on. Dad said Owen was really messed up for a while after the fire. He remembered the day Owen screamed at him on the mountain. We must have been talking for about an hour. And I didn't think about it then, but later, when I was lying in bed, it came to me. It kind of erupted in my head."

"What?"

"You and me . . . I mean, we're friends like Dad and Michael were. And last night I got into this whole thing about how I'd feel if you died. I know it sounds real creepy, but I couldn't help it. It made me feel terrible. And I thought about what Owen said about finding Dad sitting next to the statue. And I began to think about the stone boy, and—it's like it's all being repeated, Eric. You and me—Dad and Michael . . ."

"Thanks a lot!"

"What do you mean?"

"Michael died!" Eric grinned.

"Oh—I didn't mean that. It's just that . . . Well, last night I was thinking about how we hit it off so fast after you moved here. I've never had a friend like you, Eric. You know that. It's what my father said about him and Michael last night. He said they thought they could conquer the world together—that there wasn't anything they couldn't do. But then Michael died. And my father met my mother. And they had me. Except, maybe if Michael hadn't died, my father never would have met my mother. He would have gone bumming around the country, and maybe not even have gone to the state university. That's where my parents met—in their freshman year. And then

I never would have been born. And you and I never would have met. It's like Michael's death is all a part of our meeting—almost like everything is tied up together in some way."

Chris stopped talking and reached out to grasp Eric's shoulder. There was an urgency to his touch that made Eric smile.

"You, me, Owen, my father, Michael, and the stone boy are connected—like our friendship was fated!" Chris went on.

"Fated!" Eric agreed. But he was less caught up in the fated idea than Chris.

Chris's hand on his shoulder felt almost electric—as if they were alone somewhere, not standing at the street corner on the way to school. And then some kids passed by, talking, laughing. They weren't kids Eric knew, but he shivered, feeling hot and cold at the same time, and pulled away abruptly. "You realize how stupid this all is?" he said, forcing a laugh.

Chris looked as confused as Eric felt, and began fumbling to put the sketch back in his notebook.

"I mean about being fated!" Eric quickly added. The sensation of Chris's hand was still with him. He wondered if Chris had noticed it, too.

"Yeah, yeah! Crazy!" Chris said, still fumbling with the sketch.

"Here, I'll do it."

"Thanks."

"What are friends for? Fated friends, that is?"

They both laughed, and Eric elbowed Chris. "Hey, did your father mention anything about the cave?"

"I asked him. He said he and Michael used to play in it

when they were around nine and ten, kind of like it was a hide-out."

"A hide-out? Did he talk about the light or anything?"

"What light?"

"There's this light, a torch. It lights up the whole cave."

"Dad didn't mention it. And nothing about Stoneface or the Indian legends. So I didn't ask. But—I just thought of something. We never got there this summer."

"We can still go."

"You want to?"

"Yeah. Sure. Besides I haven't seen Owen in a while. How about this Saturday?"

"We have soccer practice."

"After."

"Sounds okay with me."

—

That Saturday was a warm, bright October day. The sun filtered through the thinning, autumn-colored trees as Eric and Chris made their way up Owen's road. They could hear Owen working long before they saw him. The rapid, steady beat of the hammer against the chisel stirred up memories of the summer in Eric. He'd been back only once or twice since school started.

"Do you think Owen will want to take time out to go to the cave?" Chris asked when they reached the meadow.

Eric didn't answer. His eyes were searching out the stone—even at this distance, he could see the rough shape of a new stone boy struggling from the great marble hulk. "Look," he whispered. "Look at all he's done."

Chris started into the tall grass, but Eric pulled him back.

"What's the matter?"

"Let's not bother him now. It's such a nice day. He loves to work on days like this. And he said there's a lot he wants to get done before the cold weather sets in."

"What about the cave?"

"I can find it without him."

"Are you sure?"

Eric nodded. "It's pretty near where we went walking a lot this summer. It's only hard to find if you don't know it's there. Come on, let's cut around the meadow so we don't bother him. We can stop on the way down."

"Do we climb that?" Chris asked, once Eric stopped to point out a huge rock formation jutting upwards to the sky.

"No. We crawl in here."

Chris bent down and looked into the entrance. "It's pretty dark in there."

"It won't be once I light the torch."

"How?"

"There are matches."

"And you're going to find them in the dark?"

"I sure hope so."

"I'll stay outside until you do."

"You have to come in and watch it light up. That's part of it."

Once inside, Eric stood and walked slowly across the cave, his arms extended, reaching through the darkness until he felt the walls.

"Are you still there?" Chris whispered from the entrance.

"Yeah. Just wait there."

"Did you find the matches?"

"Not yet," Eric said as he bumped into one of the

mounds of rocks. He knelt down, groping blindly. He knew Owen kept the matches near here. To his relief, he found them with no trouble. The first match broke as he struck it, but the second caught. He held it to the torch and it burst into flame.

Chris gasped.

Eric watched in wonder as the light grew brighter, the cave more vast, until it seemed to have no beginning and no end, appearing even more beautiful than he'd remembered. "What do you think?" he asked.

"It's so big. I never thought it would be so big."

"I know. Aren't the walls incredible?" Eric let his fingers glide across the smooth, wet surface.

Chris did the same, walking gingerly, as if fearing the floor might sink at any moment.

"It's like somebody came and polished them. It's always like this, Owen says."

"Your voice sounds funny. Like you're far away. And you look different."

"That's just the light. You look different, too. Nice. Kind of flickering like the flames."

"Like everything in here. The light makes the walls look like you could walk right through them. This is really a far-out place!"

"Touch the floor. It's like beach sand."

Chris let the fine pebbles flow through his fingers. Eric knelt next to him, rubbing his hand across the floor, leaving a wide arc in the sand in front of the two mounds of rocks.

"I wonder how these rocks got here?" Chris asked. "They don't look like a part of the cave."

"I don't know."

"Does Owen?"

"Maybe. I never asked him."

"Maybe my father knows."

"I bet they're some kind of sacred Indian altar." Eric smiled as he looked at Chris, bathed in the warm, soft light of the torch.

"What's so funny?"

"You. You look like I feel."

"How's that?"

"Sort of light and airy, like you might just float away."

"It must be the air in here—there's probably not enough oxygen and it's doing funny things to our heads!" Chris held out his arm. "I feel like I don't know where the light begins and I start."

"A natural high . . ."

"Does Owen have some kind of monopoly on places with natural highs?"

"What?"

"First the quarry. Now this place."

"I think maybe he does." Eric smiled. "Hey, we have to go there sometime. Maybe next summer. We could hitch. It's not all that far. Wally would probably let us camp at the quarry. All we really need is sleeping bags."

"Or we could buy a car!"

"A 1947 Plymouth!"

They laughed.

"One problem," Eric said.

"What?"

"I won't be sixteen by then."

"I will," Chris said.

"But you can't drive at night."

"So, we'll drive during the day. It stays light late in summer."

"Another problem."

"What?"

"Where do we get the bread for this car?"

"True . . ."

"Maybe we should work next summer and save up for a car?"

"Like Michael and Dad?"

"How come I always end up getting compared to Michael?"

"I didn't start it—your friend Owen did!"

"For some reason it only gives me the creeps when you do it—like death is just around the corner."

"I hope not!"

"You're not the only one!"

Chris picked up one of the stones from the neatly stacked mounds of rocks and, rubbing it against the palm of his hand, he said, "I'm kind of glad Owen didn't come with us. It wouldn't be the same."

"Maybe you shouldn't touch those," Eric said. "Maybe they're set up in some special way."

"Here, feel it."

Eric held it a moment and carefully replaced it.

"Worried about old Stoneface, huh?" Chris teased.

"Well, you never know!"

"We should have come to the mountain more this summer."

"I suggested it. You just never wanted to."

"I guess not. I don't know why . . . Well, I guess I always thought I'd feel like a third wheel or something with you and Owen and all your life-in-the-stone stuff."

"So you came on your own, right?"

"What?"

"When Owen and I were at the quarry, that's when you came to the mountain, right?" He was joking, but Chris didn't laugh. Instead, Eric saw Chris's face and body tense. "You okay?" he asked finally.

Chris half-nodded, half-shrugged, staring silently ahead.

"You sure?"

Without turning to Eric, Chris burst out, "There are things I didn't tell you about that night."

"What night?"

"When I came to the mountain."

"Hey, what did you do? Bring a can of spray paint and chicken out at the last minute?"

"It's no joke, Eric—I didn't go to Bauer's. I never even called him. I came right to the mountain . . . to see the stone boy. I knew I was going to go as soon as you told me about the trip. I was planning to go that day, but it was too hot, so I waited until after supper."

"So? I don't understand. What's wrong with that?"

Chris sighed. He looked in pain.

"You're not making sense," Eric said edgily—a part of him not wanting Chris to go on.

"Eric, do you ever think about you and me? I mean . . ." Chris turned to him, and immediately looked away.

Eric froze inside. He knew what Chris meant. He'd known the morning they walked to school and Chris had reached out to him. And maybe he'd known before that. But now it scared him. It was one thing to think about another guy like that—not even think, just feel it someplace deep inside. It was another thing to talk about it. *Don't say any more, Chris! Don't tell me!* he screamed in silent anguish, thinking he should run from the cave. But he said nothing. He didn't move. He sat watching, almost mesmerized, as Chris picked up one of the smooth, black rocks again, and rubbed it nervously in the palm of his hand.

"There's something about the stone boy, Eric. It's the marble . . . It's—I don't know. He's really beautiful . . ."

Don't, Chris! I don't want to hear!

"And I touched him," Chris said softly, so softly Eric could have easily blocked out his words. But he didn't. Too many feelings were exploding inside of him, breaking free, out of control—and he wasn't sure he could or even wanted to hold them back.

"I only touched his face," Chris was saying. "And his arm and hand. I held his hand . . . I just stood there, holding his hand. And I was thinking about you and me and all the good times we have. And I was thinking about how much—oh, God, I don't know. It was so crazy. I didn't even realize all I was thinking, Eric. I . . ." And he didn't go on.

"It's important to touch the stone, Chris. Owen always says that," Eric heard himself saying, perfectly calmly. He couldn't believe he'd said that. And he couldn't believe he could sound so calm when he was going crazy inside.

Chris turned to him, looking confused. "That's not what I meant."

Eric nodded. "I know what you meant." He swallowed and closed his eyes, thinking, *Why can't we just be friends? Why can't we just like each other? Why do I feel like this? Oh, God, I have to keep calm. We have to get out of here.* But when he started to speak, unexpected words spilled out of him. "I know what you're feeling . . ."

There was a long silence, and finally Chris said, "I

didn't think you knew. I never thought you did. Sometimes when I'd think about you and me, I'd think—I'd think if Eric ever knew what I was feeling, he'd hate me . . ."

Chris's voice was so soft and small, Eric had to look at him to make sure he was still there. When he did, the light in the cave seemed to intensify. It reflected off Chris's body as had the sun that day on the small rocky island in the middle of the reservoir when they had lain so close, touching without touching, burning, sweating, in the hot summer sun.

"There's nothing that could ever make me hate you, Chris," he said.

Chris half-smiled, spreading his hands nervously across the sandy floor, making another arc in front of the mounds of rocks. Eric did the same, and as he did, their hands touched. They stayed touching, motionless.

"Maybe we should go," Chris finally said.

"You want to?"

"I don't know. I don't know anything anymore."

"I know what you mean."

"What do you want to do?"

"What do you want to do?"

Chris swallowed hard. The sound echoed through the silence of the cave. "I know what I want to do, but I'm not sure what you want to do, I guess. Do you want to stay or what?"

"We're here," Eric said, amazed he managed to get the words out. His heart was pounding so hard, he could hear it.

Chris's hand tightened around his. It was as cold, damp and uncertain as his own. "I'm scared," Eric heard someone say. He wasn't sure whether it was Chris's voice, or his own or a voice in his mind.

Suddenly Chris was smiling, almost laughing to himself.

"What's so funny?"

"I was just thinking—do you think *this* could be the spirit of Stoneface?"

"You're . . . No!" Eric burst out laughing. *Only Chris—in this whole world, only Chris would say that now!*

And as if his body had a will of its own, Eric felt himself reaching toward Chris, moving closer until they touched. They held on to each other tightly, almost afraid to move. It all seemed so crazy—and not crazy at all. Chris's hand moved tentatively across his shoulder; and as Eric's face brushed against Chris's the light from the torch seemed to explode, fracturing into brilliant crystals of color, surrounding them, lifting them, joining them. And they drifted together into the shimmering wonder of the cave.

☰

"Eric? You okay?"

"Yeah . . ." Eric's voice was barely more than a whisper. He wrapped his arms more tightly around his legs, trying to make himself as small as possible. The wonder of the cave no longer seemed inviting or exciting. It scared him.

"You sure?" Chris asked, touching him.

Eric closed his eyes, almost cringing. How could he feel so cold and empty when only moments before holding Chris had felt so right, so warm, so good? "We better go," he said, getting up without looking at Chris. And as he put out the light, he wished he could disappear with it into the blackness.

He felt awkward and embarrassed as they emerged from the cave into the daylight. Chris's happiness, the way he looked at him and reached to touch him still, to be close as they walked down the mountain, made Eric want to run—but he didn't know who he wanted to run from more: Chris or himself—or Owen. *What if Owen sees us? Will he guess? Owen always talks about loving, but if he knew about this . . .* The thought terrified him. He felt confused, frightened and very much alone.

By the time they reached the bottom of the mountain, Chris had fallen into Eric's mood. They rode wordlessly to town—the trip seemed endless. The silence hung heavily between them. Eric kept slowing down, hoping Chris would speed off without him. But he never did. He'd turn, as if to check that Eric was still there, then pedal slowly on.

When they reached Eric's house, Eric expected Chris to keep riding; but as Eric started into the driveway, Chris called to him, "I'll see you Monday. Okay? I'll meet you at the usual time?"

Eric nodded, afraid if he spoke his voice might shatter. There was a long, terrible silence. Then Chris sped suddenly away.

Eric felt torn by a yearning, a desperate need to reach out to Chris, to call after him, "I'm sorry!" He turned around, but it was too late. Chris was already disappearing around the corner, leaving Eric alone with a silence that almost choked him. As the week passed, the loneliness and silence grew worse, keeping a deathlike grip on his emotions, locking his feelings inside him where they grew more dark and frightening each day until he froze whenever he saw Chris. And he woke up each morning hoping to find Chris didn't matter to him anymore.

He didn't go to soccer practice with Chris the next Saturday or wait for him when practice was over. Instead, he left right away. Chris caught up with him at the other end of the soccer field.

"We have to talk, Eric."

"There's nothing to talk about."

"Oh, come on . . ."

They were alone at the far end of the field, and Eric stopped abruptly and turned to Chris. "Come on, what?" he demanded. "Maybe it's okay for you. You can handle it. I can't."

"How do you know what I can handle? How do you even know what I'm thinking? We haven't really talked for a week . . ."

"There's nothing to talk about, except . . ." Eric couldn't help himself. He glared coldly at Chris. "I just want you to know something—I'm not a fag!" And he walked away.

Chris pulled him to a stop. "Eric . . ."

"I don't want to talk about it!"

"We have to."

"Not here."

"Everyone's gone. We can sit over in the bleachers. Come on, Eric—I can't stand what's happening . . ."

Eric knew he couldn't stand it either. He couldn't stand feeling numb and scared and alone anymore. But if he didn't feel those things, he wasn't sure what he'd feel; and that scared him even more. He shook his head. "I don't know."

"It's not going to kill you to talk."

"Okay—but I don't have much time. I got things to do."

They walked in silence to the bleachers.

"I just don't want our friendship to break up over this, that's all," Chris said as they sat down.

"It won't."

"It already is."

Eric looked quickly away.

"What do you think?" Chris went on. "If we're seen together, suddenly everyone's going to know? The word 'fag' is going to be burned into our foreheads?"

Eric felt himself cringe. The word sounded ugly. And he burst out, "Why can't we just be friends? Just ordinary friends like everyone has friends?"

"Because it's never been ordinary . . ."

"It was the cave, that's all! It never would have happened except for the stupid place! God, I wish I'd never gone there!"

"That's not true and you know it. If it hadn't happened at the cave, it would have been someplace else. There were hundreds of times this summer it could have happened and it didn't!"

"Speak for yourself."

"Oh, come on! How about that day we were riding out to Grosset Lake and we got lost and were just kidding around by that pond? Or the day we swam out to those rocks in the reservoir? Or plenty of nights when we were just hanging around with nothing to do. Don't tell me you never thought of it!"

"No, I never did!"

"That's not what you said in the cave."

"It's what I'm saying now."

"You're lying!"

Eric knew Chris was right. And, more than that, he knew his feelings for Chris hadn't changed. The difference was those feelings had a name now—a name which caused him to fear what he loved most about their friendship—the joy he felt from their closeness. Without thinking, he found himself asking the question he'd agonized over for the past week: "Would you do it again?"

After a long silence, Chris said, "I think so. With you . . ."

"I couldn't! Ever!" Eric insisted, loudly, forcefully.

Chris winced, as if he'd been punched.

"I didn't mean it like that. I'm sorry . . ."

"Hey, man—there's nothing to be *sorry* for!" Chris shot up as he spit out the words. "Except don't lie! I mean, God, Eric! How can you sit there and lie after everything? How can you tell me you didn't feel what was going on all summer? Because I know you did. And I know that . . ." He hesitated. "That when we were together—it wasn't bad!"

Eric didn't answer. He sat with his head bent, unable to look at Chris; but he could feel Chris glaring at him. "Why don't you just go," Eric finally said. "I told you—I told you I didn't want to talk about it . . ."

But Chris didn't leave. He sat down next to Eric again. As he did, Eric covered his face with his hands and sighed. "Oh, God, Chris—why is everything so confused in my head? I don't know what I think anymore . . ."

"Don't you see, Eric?" Chris said gently. "It doesn't ever have to happen again. The cave can always be, well—just be something good, that's all. Just something good."

Eric wanted to answer Chris. He wanted to say, *Yeah, me, too—that's how I feel, too.* But the words wouldn't come out. He was held back by his fear of what loving Chris meant. Gay, queer, fag—the words loomed threateningly before him. And he screamed in his mind, *You're words. Only words! You don't have anything to do with Chris and me!* As he did, he broke free for a moment, recapturing the feelings he had for Chris in the cave when they were close, touching, before he thought of the world finding them out. *Just something good—it was something good. It is something good. Better than good . . .* But when he looked up at Chris, the world began closing in on him again, and all he could say was, "You know, I really don't have anything to do this afternoon."

Chris smiled. "I didn't think so."

"You want to do something?"

"Sure. You want to get something to eat? I'm starved."

"I don't think I have any money."

"That's okay. I have enough for a couple slices of pizza . . ."

But they didn't leave right away. They sat a while longer. Neither of them spoke; and the silence settled softly between them, calming them, giving them something to share again.

As the weeks went by, the memory of the cave stopped causing Eric pain. He felt himself easing into his old friendship with Chris; but he felt he could never go back to Owen's—that Chris and the cave kept him from going. Yet he'd stopped going to the mountain a while before, and if Owen hadn't come over one day about a month later—it was Eric's birthday—Eric might have gone on blaming his loving Chris for his loss of Owen . . .

Eric was home alone, baby-sitting for Buddy. It was Buddy who saw Owen coming.

"Hey, Eric, there's that funny man outside."

"What funny man?"

"You know—Stoneman."

"Stoneman?"—*Owen!* He hurried to the window to see Owen walking up the front porch with a present in his arms. Even so, Eric jumped when the bell rang.

"Happy Birthday!" Owen greeted him, handing him the present.

"Gee, thanks, Owen. Thanks a lot!" he exclaimed. And he didn't know what to say next.

Owen smiled. "May I come in?"

"Sure, of course! Nobody's home but Buddy and me, but Mom and Dad should be back soon. They're just in town, shopping. I could make some coffee."

"No coffee, thanks anyway. I'd just like to come in for a while."

"Aren't you going to open your present?" Buddy asked. "What did you get?"

"Give me a chance, creep!" Eric read the card first, written in Owen's flowing script. *To my dearest friend, Eric. May next year be filled with all the joy this summer has given me. Happiest of birthdays. With love, Owen.* Putting the card safely in his pocket, Eric tore open the wrappings. "A soccer ball! Fantastic!"

"I hope it's not too late. The season must be over by now."

"It is for us since we didn't make the finals! But there's always next year!"

"I remember your saying you needed a new one."

"I do. Mine is really shot. Thanks a lot, Owen." He could feel Owen watching him, studying him; and when their eyes met, Eric looked away, embarrassed. He'd never felt that way with Owen before.

"Forgive me. I'm staring. It's just that you've changed so, Eric. When was the last time I saw you?"

"I don't know! Too long! I'm sorry. I've been meaning to come out, but with soccer and school and—there's always something. How's the stone boy coming?"

"He's coming along well, very well—at least I thought so until now."

"What do you mean?"

"Could you get me some paper? Perhaps we could sit and talk while I do some sketching."

"Sure!" Eric said, glad for a chance to get away for a moment, almost wishing Owen would be gone when he came back downstairs. But Owen was waiting for him in the living room. "Look, I'm really sorry about not coming out to see you," Eric said nervously.

"Why? I could have come to see you, too. And I haven't. I stay holed up on that mountain. And come winter, it'll be even worse. I'll hibernate as always. That's why I was thinking—let's make a date. How about next Saturday? We'll have a day of it, like in the summer—starting with breakfast!"

"Well, you sure? I mean, what if it's nice out and you want to work or something . . ."

"Eric, my dearest friend! When was the last time I saw you?"

Eric shrugged. "I don't know."

"I do. It was sometime in September, early September, I believe. And here it is, almost Thanksgiving. That makes it at least two months. And with you so busy and me so busy—we'll never get to see each other unless we make a date."

Eric was beginning to feel glad Owen had come after all. "You're right," he said.

"Good. Now tell me, what have you been up to lately? How's school?"

"Making the soccer team was great, even though we didn't do so hot."

"Did Chris make the team, too?"

Eric nodded.

"How is he?"

"Fine, fine. The same old Chris. School is pretty much a drag though. French isn't too bad, but chemistry's a total failure . . ." Eric went on talking until he realized Owen wasn't listening. He stopped suddenly, in the middle of a sentence.

"Your face is so much thinner," Owen said, leaning forward, gently outlining Eric's face with his hand as he spoke. "Your cheekbones are much more prominent . . . and your nose is broader. Your lips, too. Only your eyes haven't changed, I'm happy to say. But everything else has—your body has filled out. You're not a boy anymore!"

"If anyone else but you talked like this!" Eric exclaimed, and he couldn't help smiling. He could feel himself caught up by Owen again.

"Yes, I know—I'm probably embarrassing you. But that's the price you pay for having a sculptor as a friend. You can't escape the sculptor's eye! I like this new you very much. But you realize what it means?"

"No!"

"Changes in the stone boy. Here I've been cursing this cold autumn we've been having, but perhaps it's a blessing in disguise. It's kept me from working outside. If I had, I might not have been able to put this new you into the stone!"

When Eric's parents came home, Mrs. Nicholson insisted that Owen stay for lunch. It was a friendly, comfortable time. Owen sketched as they talked. And every now and again, he would glance at Eric and smile, as if they shared a secret. And Eric couldn't help feeling they did.

Later, Eric stood waving as Owen backed the jeep, sputtering and rumbling, out of the driveway. "Thanks for the birthday present!"

"I'll see you next Saturday!"

"You bet!" Eric shouted, tossing the ball into the air and heading it halfway across the yard.

Buddy came running toward him, scooping up the ball before Eric could get it. "Can we play?" he asked.

"Not now, kid. I got to go see Chris."

Chris was in the driveway, working on his bike with his back toward Eric. Taking aim, Eric shot the ball into the air. "Perfect!" he shouted as it landed on target, bouncing off Chris's head.

Chris jumped up. "You moron! I've been trying to get the gear working for the past hour. And I almost had it!"

"You need my expert help."

"As a matter of fact, I came over before to get it, but I saw you had company."

"You could have come in."

"I wasn't sure. Besides, I had my bike lying in pieces all over the driveway."

"He came to give me a birthday present. The soccer ball."

"No kidding?" Chris asked, picking it up. "It's a nice one."

"I'm going out to see Owen next Saturday. He said he's done some work on the new stone boy, but he needs to do more sketching."

Chris nodded and threw the ball to Eric.

"Do you realize how long it's been since I've been out there?"

"I have a pretty good idea—I was with you!"

Eric twirled the ball into the air. "I guess we never quite got around to stopping in on Owen that day!"

"Now there's an understatement! I can just see the scene. 'Oh, so nice to see you boys,' Owen would say. 'And where are you coming from?' And you'd say, 'The cave.' And he'd say, 'The cave! How interesting! Did you have a good time?' And you'd say . . ."

"Okay, okay—I get the picture!" Eric had to smile as he kicked the ball to Chris. They dribbled it back and forth a while, and Eric asked, "You still think about the cave?"

"Yeah . . . You?"

Eric nodded. "Sometimes it seems like it never happened."

"I know what you mean. And other times . . . Well, I think about it, you know . . ."

Eric kicked the ball again, and it shot sideways out of the yard, into the street. "Hey, it's rolling downhill!" he exclaimed.

"I'll get it!"

Eric followed Chris to the street and, as he turned his head, the late afternoon sun reflected off the sideview mirror of a parked car, exploding into fragments of light, blinding him. He shivered and blinked. The light grew stronger, sweeping through his body.

"I got it!" Chris shouted, running toward him, seeming to emerge from the light. "I got it!"

Chris threw the ball and Eric caught it, booting it high into the air. As he looked up, his eye caught the reflection of the sunlight again—and the ball disappeared somewhere beyond the brightness.

"What a kick!" Chris shouted.

Eric waited till the ball reappeared. "It's just the light," he said.

"What light?"

"The sunlight! It reflected off the car mirror over there and blinded me for a minute."

"The sunlight, huh?" Chris grinned.

"Yeah, the sunlight. You want to make something of it?"

They laughed together.

"You know something?" Chris asked.

"What?"

"Light will never be the same for me . . ."

Dusk on the Mountain

Eric sat close to the open stove, staring at the softly glowing flames. The words, *Just the light, huh?* echoed in his mind, and he smiled. For a while those words had been a code between Eric and Chris. Whenever they heard or saw something they didn't believe, they'd say, "Just the light, huh?" *We'd jump on it, to see which of us would say it first. I wonder if Chris remembers. Even if we saw a light that was slightly odd—like a car with only one headlight, one of us would have to say, "Just the light, huh?" . . . Tonight at the party—Tony always has those crazy strobe lights—"Just the light, Chris. Just the light, huh?"*

The party made him think of the time, and he glanced at his watch. It was almost two-thirty—and still no sign of Owen. After stoking the fire, he went to look outside. The windows were thick with ice, and he opened the door. *What a place. What an incredible place. I'd forgotten,* he thought, scanning the silent meadow. The stone people seemed one with the windswept snow. He put on his jacket and gloves, and started toward the garden.

The smiling Celia, old Celia, Nothingness, the flawed stone boy, the new stone boy—he brushed the snow off all of them, almost forgetting about the crouching Michael, who was completely covered. When they were all swept clean, he stood back to look at them. "Hello, all!" He smiled, trying to remember the last time he'd been here. It was hard to recall exactly . . .

But I came out a lot that first winter—well, maybe not a lot, but still I came out. And then it was in summer—no, it was fall when Owen finished you . . . Eric thought, looking at the new stone boy. *School had already started. And Owen met me after school. "He's done!" he shouted. "Finally finished! Come see him!"*

A thin layer of new snow was sticking to the sculpture. Eric brushed it off the stone boy's head and nose, then took off his glove, rubbing his hand against the stone face, letting his fingers slide across the smooth, cold marble cheek to the neck, the shoulder, the arm, finally resting on the stone boy's hand . . .

After you were finished, I hardly came out at all—once

with Mom and Dad, and then . . . I've stayed away too long . . .

"He's you, Eric! Only you. You've given him life," he heard Owen say.

Eric spun around.

No one was there.

The entrance to the cave was covered with snow. Eric kicked away as much as he could and cleared the rest with his hands, then crawled inside. He knelt in the darkness a while, unsure why he'd come, for even as he'd made his way up the mountain he knew he wasn't going to find Owen in the cave. There were no signs of anyone having been this way since the first big snowfall of the winter, weeks ago. And yet, he'd kept on. Now, as he sat in the darkness, shivering, he wondered why. *This is insane. That long hike up here. It's freezing cold. And now I have to trudge back down. I just should have waited for Owen at the cabin. God, I have to get out of here. It's freezing.* But he didn't go. The black silence of the cave held him a little longer. And then there was the light. He knew he had to see the light again.

He found the matches easily, as easily as he'd found the cave in the snow. For an instant, the brightness of the flame blinded him; but as he looked around the cave, turning in a slow circle, his eyes adjusted to its glow. He gasped: Owen was sitting on the floor between the two mounds of rocks. He was leaning against the wall, a blanket wrapped around him and his old woolen cap pulled down over his ears. He looked asleep.

At first, Eric couldn't move or breathe. The gasp seemed caught in his throat, almost choking him. "Owen," he finally managed to get out. "Owen?"

Owen didn't move.

Eric walked slowly toward him, kneeling down only inches away. He watched as the light danced across Owen's face in flickering shadows, smoothing away the lines of age. His skin seemed so smooth, his features so fine—as if they'd been carved out of the stone.

"I'm here, Owen. I'm back," he whispered.

Owen didn't answer.

"Owen, I'm back. It's me, Eric," he cried, reaching out to touch him, to wake him.

But Owen couldn't be wakened. He was cold and hard, as cold and hard as the stone people.

A moan tore from inside Eric. "I've come back, Owen! You knew I'd be back! Why didn't you wait for me, Owen?" And as his cries resounded through the cave, the light seemed to lose its warmth, its glow. He shivered violently. "Why didn't you let me know? Didn't you want to see me one more time? Didn't you know I'd come back if only you asked, Owen? Why didn't you let me know?" The cold was piercing now, and he wrapped his arms tightly around himself, rocking back and forth to keep warm. "You're not dead, Owen. You can't be dead . . ." he mourned, feeling so numb, so tired. "Oh, God, Owen . . ." He cried softly. As he did, he caught sight of what appeared to be carvings on the wall above where Owen lay. He had never noticed any before, and he had to turn the light to make them out. They were words. He touched them with his fingers as he read:

ERIC—
LEAVE ME HERE WITH CELIA AND MICHAEL. THIS SMALL PLACE OF WONDER IS OURS FOR ETERNITY. I LEAVE THE REST IN YOUR CARE. I WILL BE WITH

YOU ALWAYS. TOUCH ME THROUGH THE STONE AND I WILL KNOW WHEN YOU RETURN. MAY YOUR LIFE BE FULFILLING, MY DEAREST FRIEND. MAY YOUR MIND SOAR, FOREVER FREE.

—OWEN

Eric's tears blurred his eyes, and he had to read the stone message several times before it made sense.

"Eric, is that you?"

Eric looked up to see Chris walking toward him from the light. He thought he was hallucinating.

"Eric?"

"Chris?" he gasped. "Is that really you?"

"What are you doing here? It's freezing." And then he saw Owen. "Oh, my God! He's dead!"

"How do you know?"

"What do you mean? He looks dead! Are you crazy or something?"

"Does he really *look* dead?"

"Of course! Frozen stiff. Jesus, it's lucky it happened in winter. How long have you been up here?"

"I don't know. What time is it?"

"Almost four-thirty."

"I guess I've been here a while." He shivered suddenly. "It's cold in here."

"You're not kidding. And we have a long way back to my car."

"He came here to die, Chris."

"Let's talk about it someplace else. You're freezing."

Eric barely heard Chris. He turned to Owen. "He looks so peaceful. It's hard to believe he's dead."

"We better go. It'll be dark soon."

"He knew he was dying, Chris. Look—" He showed Chris the stone message. "I don't understand why he didn't tell me—I would have . . ." But he couldn't finish. His throat tightened and tears welled up, burning his eyes. He turned from Chris, covering his face with his hands. "I'm sorry . . ." he said. "Just give me a minute."

Chris reached for him, putting his hands on Eric's shoulders. "It's okay," he said softly.

"Oh, God . . ." Eric moaned, wrapping his hands more tightly around his head, as if to force the pain and the sorrow back inside him. He didn't want Chris to see him like this. *Owen was old. Old people die.* And that summer was so long ago. Why should he still care so much?

Chris pulled Eric toward him.

"He was my friend," Eric whispered. "I don't want him to be dead . . ."

"But look what he carved on the wall—he knew you'd be back. He never doubted you'd be back. And you are. That's amazing. It's beautiful. It's all here, isn't it? He never stopped loving you."

Chris's words, his closeness, his caring, seemed to break free the sorrow inside Eric. It swept through him with such force, his whole body shook. He didn't even try to hold back the tears. He couldn't. Dropping his hands from his face, he leaned against Chris, grasping him tightly, letting himself be comforted.

"Eric, you okay?" Chris asked.

"I think so." Eric sighed, finally able to let go.

Chris looked down at Owen. "He was quite a guy. I wish I'd known him better." And gazing around the cave, he added, "It'll be strange to think of this place as a tomb."

"I think it has been for a long time."

"What do you mean?"

Eric spoke softly, hesitantly. His voice kept cracking. "I'll bet you anything those two mounds of rocks are Michael's and Celia's graves—the way they look, the way they're piled so perfectly—nobody but Owen could have done it like that."

Chris turned to the stone message. "So that's what he meant about leaving him with Michael and Celia."

"I think so."

"Are you going to close up the cave?"

"In the spring, when the ground thaws. Would you mind helping me?"

"Mind? I'm glad you asked me."

As they started to leave, Chris's foot kicked something hard. He bent down to pick it up. It was a box with Eric's name on it.

Inside were Owen's tools—the tools he had used to sculpt the stone people, the tools he had used to carve into the cave wall. Wrapped around the tools was a piece of paper, a will drawn up by a lawyer, leaving the land and all Owen's possessions, including the stone people, to Eric.

Eric knelt down next to Owen, and pulling back the blanket, he placed the tools in Owen's hands. "You'll need these, my friend . . ." he whispered, watching the flame flicker across Owen's face for the last time.

Eric and Chris hardly spoke as they ran through the snow down the mountain, racing against the setting sun. It was almost dark when they reached Chris's car, parked at the end of Old Reservoir Road.

"Whew, I wasn't sure we'd make it," Chris said. "I had

images of us spending New Year's Eve on Stoneface Mountain."

"That doesn't sound so bad."

"I'd prefer the party."

"I was thinking, maybe I won't go."

"That's what I figured."

"You think I should?"

"No—I think you should do whatever you want."

As they got in the car, Eric asked, "What about the bike?"

"We'll have to tie it onto the roof somehow." Chris started the engine. "But let's get warm first. Whatever possessed you to bike out here anyway?"

"Something about last night—something you said about mileage and getting hooked on stone people, quarries and places where the earth speaks. I guess I had to see if it was still true."

"Is it?"

Eric smiled. "You came to the cave today."

"What kind of an answer is that?"

"Remember what you once said about us? About our friendship being fated?"

"Yes, but I was fifteen when I said that. Besides, there's a very rational explanation for today. When I called you this afternoon, your mother said you'd ridden your old bike out here early this morning. She was worried. So was I. So I came out. All I had to do was follow your footsteps. They led me right to the cave."

"Just a coincidence, huh?"

Chris grinned. "Maybe. And maybe not . . ."

"Did you see the new stone boy?"

"I was following your footsteps."

"What did you think?"

"It sure brought back memories standing there—he's beautiful. He really is. Owen knew how to sculpt."

"He was an artist, wasn't he?"

"Did you ever doubt it?"

"I guess I didn't think much about it," Eric said, folding his arms across the dashboard, peering into the darkness toward the mountain. "It seemed almost magical what he did with the stone. I had the feeling it could only happen here on Stoneface Mountain. Owen said the mountain has a soul of its own and anyone who experiences it becomes a part of it, like Owen and the stone people . . ." He turned to Chris. "And you and me . . ."

Chris smiled. "The spirit of Stoneface Mountain—maybe it was with us after all."

"I think so!" Eric exclaimed, leaning back against the seat, relaxing into the growing warmth of the dimly lit car.

"Well, what do you say we get going? I have to get ready for tonight."

"Hey, Chris, I was thinking—maybe I will go tonight."

"Okay! Sounds good to me!"

"I can't promise to be the life of the party."

"You never are—so nobody will notice!" Chris laughed.

It wasn't until they were almost in town that they realized they'd left the bike leaning against Owen's jeep at the end of Old Reservoir Road.